"Are you ready?"
"Yes, we are ready."
"When are they coming?"
"Soon."
"Then will it be over?"
"Yes, it will be over. When the price is paid."

COLD REVENGE

CATHERINE CAVENDISH

Dedication

To Colin, without whom…

Acknowledgments

A massive "thank you" to Crossroad Press
for being an amazing publisher

Nadine

"God, I hate dinner parties." Nadine stretched slim legs along the sofa. "All that endless small talk with people you've never met or hardly know and wouldn't normally bother with." She brushed imaginary lint off her black Versace dress.

Her partner, Paul Kelly, lit a cigarette and stroked her smooth, tanned arm. "Nadine darling, you can't ignore Erin Dartford. She's one of the foremost fashion writers in the country. Upset her and *Vogue* will stop calling."

Nadine let him kiss her neck and nuzzle her. She closed her eyes and could feel the familiar stirrings of desire. Normally, it would only lead one way. *But not tonight. Tonight I have to go and be civil to Erin Dartford and prostitute myself for six column inches.* Nadine knew which six inches she would prefer right now but she had to stop Paul going any further. They would be late and, besides, she didn't want to ruin the Versace.

She pushed him away and stood up, noting the surprised look on his face. "Sorry Paul, but if we're going to this thing, we've got to go. I've heard Erin doesn't forgive latecomers lightly. You're likely to get leftovers."

She watched Paul check himself in the mirror as he straightened his tie and smoothed down his dark Armani suit. Nothing but the best for Paul Kelly. The best in designer wear, the trophy girlfriend on his arm ... Nadine knew he wasn't with her for her brains. If she hadn't been a model—and one whose fine-boned face graced many a *Vogue* cover—she would never have landed the Internet entrepreneur.

Nadine slipped her black-stockinged feet into the Jimmy Choos that would be giving her toes grief by ten o'clock. She checked her appearance in the mirror. Good, her makeup was still immaculate and her long, black hair shimmered in the artificial light. *Penelope Cruz, eat your heart out.* She leaned a little closer to the mirror and examined her face. Flawless. Not a blemish. No airbrushing for *her* photographs, and that was more than most of them could boast.

Paul came up behind her and put his hands on her shoulders. "We make a pretty handsome couple, don't we?" He grinned, showing expensive white teeth.

"Ever the modest one," she purred, wishing again that they didn't have to go anywhere tonight. Her longing for him was almost too great to bear, and she could feel herself tingling in places she wished he could touch, or better still, kiss … right now. But he would have to wait. Erin Dartford wouldn't.

"I wouldn't mind," Nadine said in the car as she checked her lip gloss for the third time, "but she's only been around five minutes and we all dance to her tune. She appeared from nowhere with a column in *Vogue* and suddenly she's the critic you have to impress."

"She must have paid her dues somewhere," Paul said. "Maybe she was big on the Internet, although I can't say I had ever heard of her until a couple of years ago."

She was thoughtful for a moment, then snapped her compact shut before replacing it in her purse. "Well, wherever she came from, or whoever she was before, she is certainly someone now. Gilly said if I upset Erin in any way, I could kiss good-bye to the rest of my career. Crazy the power some of these critics have."

"Your manager knows what she's talking about. You'd better listen to her."

"I'm in the car, aren't I? I'm going to her wretched dinner party, aren't I?"

"OK, OK, I'm not the bad guy here." Paul laughed.

"Sorry." Nadine meant it. She sighed. "Gilly says I should be honored. After all, Erin's never met me. Apparently that's quite unusual. She'll normally have done a feature on you before you get an invitation to the Hallowed Hall."

"The what?"

"Hallowed Hall. It's what people call the mansion where she lives and where we're going tonight. It's set in around six acres of one of the most exclusive parts of Surrey and it's a former abbey. Its real name is St. Saviour's but everyone calls it the Hallowed Hall. It's supposed to be haunted."

"Isn't everywhere in Surrey? Everywhere that's more than fifty years old at any rate."

"They had that TV program there. You know, the one fronted by the woman with the piercing scream and the parapsychologist with the weird gadgets. They heard a lot of knocking and the furniture moved around quite a bit."

"Amazing what you can do with a bit of nylon thread and a hammer, isn't it?"

Nadine smacked his arm. "Oh Paul, you're such a cynic!"

"You have reached your destination."

"Thank you, GPS," Paul said.

Nadine giggled. It always made her laugh when he talked to his SatNav. She peered out of the window. At dusk on this summer evening, the shadows were lengthening, but the dwindling sun still shed enough light to make out the detail of the mythical beasts carved on top of the stone pillars on either side of a tall pair of wrought iron gates. These slowly opened.

"Must have seen us on CCTV or something," Paul mused and looked upward, apparently searching for the camera without success.

Nadine also looked up and shivered. Strange how fierce that stone beast looked and how realistic, as if, at any moment, it might leap down and strike. *Must be the light.* Still, she couldn't wait to put some distance between them.

Ahead of them stretched a long drive and, at the end, a large illuminated house that, even from this distance, looked ecclesiastical.

Paul threw the Ferrari in gear. "OK, let's not keep the lady waiting."

As they approached, Nadine took in the large sandstone building with its many arched windows. Two flights of stone steps curved upward to a small terrace in front of an imposing entrance flanked by two narrow turrets. Each of these was carved with figures she couldn't quite make out, silhouetted against the darkening sky.

He parked and, as they stepped onto the gravel, a soft breeze played around Nadine's hair. She took Paul's hand, taking care not to trip in her five-inch heels. Without warning, her stomach turned over and, for an instant, she thought she was going to be sick. She felt as if her body was telling her to leave. The nausea was over in a flash but it unnerved her. *This is crazy. It's just a stupid dinner party.* But the inexplicable feeling of unease wouldn't go away.

Soft music wafted toward them through the open door. They stepped over the threshold, and Nadine looked around at the scene of conspicuous wealth. The abbey showed its ancient heritage in the stone facade and the worn carvings of saints, some of whose faces had long lost their detail through the actions of wind, sun, and rain.

The interior was light and airy. Nadine recognized the entrance hall in which they were standing, from a feature in *Hello* magazine some months before. The room was vast, its pale lemon walls hung with old oil paintings depicting, she presumed, former abbots. A giant marble table took pride of place in the center of the black-and-white tiled floor. Three intricately carved cherubs appeared to be holding it up, and its surface was covered in orange roses, which gave off a heady scent that filled the hall. Above them, an enormous crystal chandelier glittered. Its many pendants tinkled gently in the slight breeze from outside.

Two other couples stood at opposite ends of the hall, sipping champagne. That was strange; Nadine was sure she and Paul had arrived on time. Maybe everyone else planned to be fashionably late, although that was somewhat at odds with Erin's famed insistence on punctuality.

"You must be Nadine Cornwall. How lovely to meet you at last." Erin looked exactly like her photographs. Tall, thin to the point of emaciation, she was one of those women whose age was impossible to guess. She could have been anywhere between thirty-five and sixty. Her hair was a helmet of black, her eyes heavy lidded, vivid blue, and chilling. Her lips were a slash of scarlet, matched by her long nails, but she was dressed from head to toe in black. Nadine had never seen Erin pictured in anything else.

Erin was waiting to shake Nadine's hand, so she tore her eyes away from Erin's compelling gaze. Her hands were covered in opulent rings, the most stunning of which was an enormous ruby that reminded Nadine of a Pope's ring she had once seen in an old film. *Maybe she expects me to kiss the bloody thing.*

Apparently not, and Nadine allowed the older woman to take her hand, immediately wishing she hadn't. Erin's grasp was dry, and her hands claw-like. Nadine was relieved when it was safe to withdraw her hand. "Pleased to meet you, Miss Dartford."

"Oh please, call me Erin, everyone does."

But not because they like you. They fear you. Nadine wished Erin would stop staring.

As if reading Nadine's mind, Erin turned her attention to Paul. "And you must be Nadine's husband?"

"Partner." He took her hand and kissed it lightly.

Nadine flinched involuntarily and hoped that Erin hadn't noticed, but the thought of Paul's lips in contact with that dry, dusty hand brought on another wave of nausea.

"I'm Paul Kelly."

"Of course. You made a fortune out of those clever little websites that show us how we can all save money if only we follow your advice."

Paul smiled and Nadine watched the exchange, fascinated. Erin's returning smile stayed firmly planted on her lips while, in her eyes …

"You have no idea what is going to happen to you. You came from nothing and you shall return to nothing."

"Nadine! Are you all right?"

She jumped. Paul was shaking her arm. Erin had moved on to another couple.

"I thought you were going to pass out. You went so pale."

She stared at him. "I have no idea, Paul. Maybe it's low blood sugar. I really don't know. What did I do?"

Paul smiled. "Nothing really. I don't think Erin noticed. Her attention was diverted by Maggie O'Donnell over there." He nodded toward the famous crime writer whose latest bestseller Nadine had recently enjoyed. "She was talking to me and I caught you swaying slightly. You were staring at Erin and growing paler by the second. I really thought you were going to faint. What was it?"

Nadine searched her brain for an answer but could find none. She'd heard a voice in her head but she couldn't remember what it had said.

"I don't know, Paul. All I want is to go home. Now."

Paul moved closer to her. "Nadine, you can't. You know that. She would be offended and you would be committing career suicide. Who knows? I might even be affected by the fallout. Come on and pull yourself together. It's a bit warm in here and you haven't eaten anything since breakfast."

"Gilly said I needed to lose a couple of pounds."

"You do not need to lose a couple of pounds. Hell, you make Ariana Grande look overweight."

A waiter appeared with a tray of champagne and Paul handed her a glass. Nadine's hands were shaking, but she did her best to steady them and took a large swig, not surprised to find the bubbly was good quality and perfectly chilled. She recalled how, five years ago, she wouldn't have known good champagne from a glass of cider. But that was before she became famous. Before … *No, I don't want to remember that. Not now. Not ever.*

Paul was looking at her, curiosity in his gaze.

Her stomach heaved again. "I need to find a bathroom," she said, handing him her empty glass and hurrying away, aware that he was following her every step.

The waiter directed her out of the hall, down a long, arched passageway. Hobbled by her heels, Nadine removed her shoes and, as she sped past the tapestry-covered walls, was vaguely aware of scenes depicting heroic battles between good and evil. She located the door she needed and opened it, shutting and locking it behind her. She leaned against it, sweat beading her brow.

The room contained an old-fashioned toilet and a dressing table with a mirror over it. Ornate gilt wall lights cast a muted glow over dark red wallpaper, giving it a Gothic air. She dropped her shoes on the floor, took a tissue from a box on the table, and gently dabbed her forehead and upper lip, closing her eyes and fanning herself to cool down. Her stomach seemed to be doing somersaults.

"Nadine."

She jumped. Her eyes shot open. The voice had been in her ear. "Who is it?" she called.

No one replied.

I'm going mad. Paul's right. I must eat properly. I'm hallucinating because my blood sugar's dropped too low.

"Nadine. *You know who I am.*"

Terror overwhelming her, she grabbed her shoes, unlocked the door, and wrenched it open. In the passageway, she leaned against the wall, panting.

That voice. She recognized that voice. But it couldn't be. She must have imagined it. The hunger. Maybe even the heat. After all, the temperature had soared today.

Maggie O'Donnell went by, a strange expression on her face, but Nadine was barely aware of her. She was slipping away. Gradually the passageway throbbed, and started to fade as if a mist was descending.

"Where on earth have you been?" Paul asked. "You've been gone nearly half an hour. I was worried you'd lost your nerve and run away."

"No, nothing like that. I've just been back a long time in my life and met someone I haven't seen in a long time."

Paul looked around at Erin and the two other couples in the room. "Who was that?"

"Me," she replied.

Gary

"Look out, you're going to hit that child!"

Gary Duncan's car lurched. He heard the awful thud of a speeding vehicle hitting a body. Then silence.

"I told you that you were going to hit that child and now he's dead. He's lying under the wheels of your car and you killed him. What are you going to do?"

He woke up in a sweat and sat bolt upright in bed. The moon snaked silvery rays into the cool bedroom, and he looked at the sleeping shape next to him. His wife, Melissa. Thank God he hadn't woken her this time. Lately, she seemed to have been having enough problems of her own trying to sleep.

Pushing the duvet aside, Gary sat on the edge of the bed, heart pounding. He hadn't had that nightmare for years. And a decade had passed since that terrible night.

He stood and fumbled his way to the bathroom in the dark. He didn't want Melissa coming in to see him as he knew he must look, so once inside, he locked the door and switched on the light. One glance in the mirror told him he was right. His sandy hair was disheveled. His eyes were red rimmed and troubled, while the graying stubble on his chin aged him by a good ten years. She would know straightaway that the nightmares had returned and would start asking him those endless questions again.

Who? Where? What? When? And the one he always had the greatest problem with: *Why?* He was sure Melissa was convinced there was some deep, repressed memory at the heart of his sleepless nights.

But only Gary knew the truth.

One day—ten years, five months, two weeks, and three days ago— he had killed someone, and the memory of it was as clear as it always had been.

On a cold January evening, he had stopped for a couple of drinks with the guys from work.

"Go on, have one more. It's my round." Harry had insisted.

Gary had hesitated at first, knowing he was probably already over the limit, but it was Harry's round. Harry, who never put his hand in his pocket, was offering to buy him a drink.

"Oh, why not?" Gary had agreed. A half hour and two shots of whiskey later, he had unlocked his car and set off for home.

The rain was turning to sleet on a dark, cold night. He'd glanced down at the clock on the dashboard. Just after six thirty. He'd be home by seven, would put a microwave meal in the oven for twenty minutes, and settle down to watch the football.

Pulling away from traffic lights, he'd turned left down a side street when he was distracted by his cell phone ringing. He'd taken his eye off the road for a second to see who was calling. He hadn't recognized the number.

That's when he'd felt the thud.

Christ! He knew he'd hit something, maybe a dog or a cat. He pulled over and cut the engine, shoved his cell phone into his coat pocket, and opened the car door. Behind him on the deserted street, a lump lay on the glistening tarmac, illuminated by a streetlamp.

Gary dashed over and, to his horror, he saw that the lump was a young boy, probably no more than twelve years old. He was very still.

Gary stared at him, willing him to open his eyes. His hands shaking, he felt the boy's wrist and neck for a pulse, but could find nothing.

The horror of what he had done hit him, and he started to panic. Had anyone seen him? Scanning all around him, there was no sign of anyone. He knew he should call an ambulance … and the police. He also knew that he was well over the blood alcohol limit.

He would lose his driving license and without his license, he would lose his job as a sales executive.

Thoughts raced through his head. He would never get a decent job again, and he had won his company's Top Sales Executive award six months running. His salary and bonuses put him well into a higher tax bracket. He'd lose that too.

He looked down at the still figure, lightly covered with sleet, which was rapidly turning into snow. The boy had to be dead.

Another awful truth hit him.

The boy was dead.

Gary had killed him.

He'd been drinking … he could be prosecuted for manslaughter.

He could be jailed for years.

Gary hesitated, and then stood.

No sign of anyone around. Most of the houses were boarded up. The area was prime for redevelopment—if any money was around for that— and God alone knew what the boy had been doing here in the first place. Maybe he had been on an errand for his mother and had taken a shortcut.

What the hell does it matter? I have to decide what to do.

Maybe he had only seconds. At any moment, someone could come down the street. Another driver, a pedestrian or, God forbid, a police patrol car, and his decision would be made for him.

He reached in his pocket for his cell phone. *No, they'll be able to trace the call. They'll know it's me.*

Gary made his decision. *I'm sorry, kid, I never meant for this to happen, but you're out of it now and I've still got my life to lead.*

He raced back to his car and got out of there as fast as possible. Back on the main road, he saw a public call box and stopped next to it, intending to call an ambulance. But he didn't know the name of the street where he had left the boy.

Again, he hesitated. Should he even call at all?

It would be so easy to start up the engine and go home, inspect the damage, and get the car fixed tomorrow.

He could forget about it and get on with his life. Someone would find the body. Sooner or later.

He sat for a few moments as the cars shot past him. People finishing their day's work, looking forward to getting out of the wet and cold into their cozy homes, tucked up with a nice glass of wine or playing with their children.

Would the boy's mother be starting to wonder where he was? Would she be going out to look for him?

Yes, that was it. The boy's parents would find him. They would know where he was going and would retrace his steps. *I'm so sorry for your loss.*

Gary had reached for the keys and turned on the ignition. Fifteen minutes later, he arrived home and put his car in the garage with the door firmly locked.

In the morning, he called in sick and, dressed in jeans and a thick sweater against the biting wind, went out through the kitchen door and into the garage.

The car had sustained remarkably little damage, considering that the impact had killed a young boy. Volvos were said to be built like tanks, and Gary decided that was not an urban myth. The dent would need fixing or, at worst, the bumper could be replaced. Gary had peered at it closely. No sign of blood. From what he could see, contact with a wall could have done it. In fact, almost anything substantial could have caused that bump. And he hadn't been speeding, either.

The boy had been unlucky. That was what had happened. The roads had been a little icy, so maybe he'd slipped and hit his temple. Catch *that* the wrong way and it would take relatively little to kill him outright.

Gary called a garage he had never used before, a little out of town where no one would know him. Best not to chance it.

When Gary got there, the mechanic seemed perfectly satisfied with the explanation.

"I did some shopping, came out of the supermarket, and there it was."

"Probably a shopping cart. Or maybe a car with a tow bar reversed into you. That happens a lot." The young man in dirty blue overalls fingered the dent with oil-slicked hands.

Gary found himself holding his breath.

"Yeah, we can fix that for you. We'll stick a new bumper on it. I'll order one. Should be ready in a couple of days. If you leave your number, we'll give you a call."

Gary gave him his cell phone number. "And your name?"

Gary hesitated. "Jim. It's Jim Westwood."

The mechanic wrote it down. "OK. How are you getting home? Do you want me to run you anywhere?"

"Oh, no, that's fine. I'll take the bus," he said hurriedly, with no clue where the bus stop was or even which one to catch to transport him the fifteen miles back to his home.

The mechanic was about to point him in the right direction when a pretty girl with long, straight blonde hair emerged from the office.

"Hey, Melissa!" the mechanic called. The girl smiled and sauntered over. "Show Mr. Westwood where the bus stop is, will you? He's going back to Medford."

"Sure." She smiled at Gary, treating him to a display of even white teeth and violet eyes.

Back home, Gary had turned on the TV to watch the local news, feeling as if the previous evening's horrors had never happened. He was almost beginning to believe he had imagined it, apart from the damage to his car. After all, he had consumed far more whiskey than he should have.

A photograph flashed onto the screen. "Police are trying to trace the whereabouts of a hit and run driver who left a seriously injured boy to die on a freezing street in the Walworth area of Medford yesterday evening."

He'd jumped to his feet.

"Eleven-year-old Patrick Morgan had been on his way to a local shop when he appears to have been struck by a passing vehicle. His mother, Stephanie Morgan, went looking for him when he failed to return home and discovered him lying on the street. She called an ambulance but he was pronounced dead at the scene. There were no witnesses to the accident and anyone with any information is asked to contact their local police station or ring Medford Police on ..."

Gary couldn't bear to watch anymore. He switched off the television. Every muscle in his body twitched. His hands shook.

He should turn himself in. But the police would contact local garages asking if any vehicles had been brought in for repair.

Gary prayed he'd struck lucky.

He stayed out sick for the rest of the week, genuinely too stressed to concentrate on anything except the awful crime he had committed. Every time the doorbell rang, he jumped and, on one such occasion, he startled two Jehovah's Witnesses by the warmth of his greeting. Little could they know his kindness had been the result of pure relief that they weren't a pair of police officers.

Again and again over the next few days, he'd come close to handing himself in. He'd been so sure the police would be waiting for him when he went to collect his car that he dressed in a suit and tie. He felt more confident, better equipped to deal with whatever befell him.

The girl he had met, Melissa, greeted him with a certain reserve that set him wondering if she had guessed what had really happened to his car. But her expression hadn't given anything away, and she'd been polite enough.

She'd been in charge of the accounts and general office work. The garage was small but busy. The place had at least three mechanics and there'd been about ten cars lined up, waiting for varying degrees of attention. It buzzed with activity, with drills whining, machinery clanking, and metal clattering on cement as a wrench was dropped or discarded. A radio blasted.

Melissa's quiet air of sophistication seemed out of place in such a masculine environment. Despite all his fears, Gary had felt aroused as he scanned her long, slim legs, short skirt, and clingy mohair sweater. Garages were cold places and he had imagined her nipples, taut and erect from the chill. *This is absurd. How can I be turned on at a time like this?*

He paid her in cash to avoid questions about his name.

And he asked her out. Risky, but he hadn't been able to help himself. He had to have her. After an initial hesitation, to his amazement she'd said yes.

Less than a year later, they'd married. Gary was finally beginning to feel that the horror of that awful night was over. The story had gradually faded from the TV and press. Evidently no one had connected the dent in his bumper with the accident. No one had ever been charged with the crime. He'd tried to push the memory of it all to the back of his mind.

As the weeks went by, he'd sometimes find he'd gone a whole day without thinking about it.

And he'd fallen in love with Melissa. She was perfect. Somehow he managed to convince her that he'd used a fake name because the Volvo was a company car and he hadn't wanted his boss to know that he had carelessly left the hand brake off when he stopped briefly to buy a newspaper. The car had rammed into a tree, he told her. She'd seemed to believe him, and that had been the last time they had spoken about it.

She hated working at the garage. "They're always leering at me and making dirty suggestions. Not to mention the boredom," she told him.

"Get another job. I'll help you," he said and had helped her rewrite her CV. After six months, she came home one day, beaming. "I'm going to be working as PA to the Fashion Editor of *Allegra* magazine!"

He had hugged her then and the next time and another as she worked her way up through increasingly more glossy magazines until one day, a few months ago when she announced that she'd landed the job as PA to the most influential fashion writer of them all. Erin Dartford.

As for the nightmares, Melissa had nursed him through the awful nights after they'd begun. Strangely, they hadn't started until nearly a year after the accident.

The first one had hit on their honeymoon, and it had been so vivid.

He was driving his Volvo down the deserted street but he was also sitting next to himself in the passenger seat. It was his own voice, emanating from that other Gary, that told him he was going to hit the boy. No matter how many times he dreamed it, he'd never seen the child he hit.

The first few times it happened, he awakened crying. Melissa would cradle his head and let him sob out his grief. "What's wrong? Please tell me. Let me help you."

But he hadn't. He'd said it was only a nightmare. Some nonsense his brain was manufacturing. Then they stopped. A month went by, a year and he could finally face going to bed again without worrying he was going to relive that awful night.

And then, without warning, they started again. Tonight. The night before they had to go to Erin Dartford's party. *Just what I bloody need.*

Scowling at his reflection, Gary opened the bathroom cabinet and took out a small bottle of paracetamol. His head had begun to throb, and a migraine was threatening. He held a glass beneath the sink tap and was about to turn the knob when …

A sudden noise. He stopped dead. What was it? He listened hard. There it was again.

A faint mewing. A cat. That was all. One of the neighborhood tomcats was out on the prowl and the sound was floating in through the open windows.

"Mummy. Help me! I'm lost."

His hand went limp and the glass shattered on the floor.

Maggie

"Poor Liam. You never saw any of my success, did you?" Maggie O'Donnell sighed at the smiling face in the old photograph and set its frame back onto the bookshelf. She ran her finger along the smooth polished wood, and examined it. *That stupid girl hasn't dusted properly again. She'll have to go.*

Maggie went to the Art Deco mirror hanging over the fireplace. Turning one way and the other, she patted her hair and smiled at her reflection. Her auburn, wavy hair was perfect. That new hairdresser certainly seemed to know his stuff, even if he was as camp as Liberace.

Her husband, Geoff, came into the room. "Ah, there you are. Ready to go?"

"Yes, just making last minute preparations." Maggie smiled at him.

"Let me look at you." He took both her hands in his and ran his gaze admiringly up and down her slim frame. Her dress was a Lanvin original in green silk crepe de chine and hung beautifully in a Grecian draped style, showing off her shoulders, her best features.

"That's a lovely dress. The green suits you. Shows off your hair."

"It should do. It cost a packet." Maggie kissed him lightly on the nose.

"Well, Countess Abelard will just have to do some more sleuthing, won't she?"

"Don't mock her. She's kept me in the manner to which I always wanted to become accustomed for over ten years. I'm very grateful to her, and all her blue-blooded relatives. Without her I wouldn't have had five bestsellers and two successful films."

Geoff nodded at to the photograph on the bookshelf. "Wonder what Liam would have made of it all."

Maggie avoided his eyes. "Let's go, shall we? I've heard Erin Dartford isn't wild about guests arriving late. I think she seats you below the salt or something equally humiliating."

Maggie arranged herself in the front passenger seat of their Mercedes, taking care to avoid creasing her dress. Geoff started the engine and pulled away from their mews home.

"How well do you know her?" he asked.

"Erin? I've only met her once. Funnily enough, it was at the fashion show where I bought this dress. She admired the suit I was wearing and said she was a great fan of my books. I remember she said I should come for dinner one evening. I agreed, so here we are."

"St. Saviour's Abbey, Little Hopton. Sounds like the sort of place your countess might discover a body."

She laughed. "Yes, it does rather, doesn't it? It's been featured in all the glossies. Apparently it was a ruin before she renovated it. She must have spent millions on it. It's even still got the original cloisters although I think they've been enclosed, so now they're merely long passageways with rooms running off them."

"You wouldn't think writing about women's frocks could generate enough money for that sort of home, would you?"

"Women's frocks? Geoff, we are talking about haute couture." She chuckled. "Writers like Erin Dartford can make or break a designer. Just like that." She snapped her fingers. "I have heard that even Donatella Versace quakes in her fake tan whenever she sees Erin at one of her catwalk shows."

"What a crazy world we live in," Geoff said as he turned the car into a short driveway leading to some closed gates. On his approach, they started to open. "Very grand."

The light was fading but it was still quite warm. This Surrey mansion seemed a world away from the bustle of Knightsbridge where they lived. As Geoff drove slowly up the long gravel drive, Maggie looked at the trees on either side, tall and barely moving in the lightest of evening breezes. In front of them, growing larger as they approached, the imposing abbey. Nicknamed "The Hallowed Hall," it certainly lived up to its name, majestic and illuminated against the evening sky.

Geoff pulled up in front of the abbey, and Maggie took his hand as she inched her way out of the car, grateful she'd picked low-heeled evening sandals. Walking in anything higher on the gravel would have been precipitous at best.

Reaching the stone steps, Maggie lifted her skirt and ascended, careful to avoid snagging her heels in her hem. The front door was open, and light from the entrance hall flooded the small terrace at the top of the steps. She could hear soft music. Strauss maybe.

"I wonder how many she's invited. I don't know anyone else who has come to one of her dinner parties, so I've no idea what we've let ourselves in for."

"Too late to back out now. Someone's seen us. Is that her?"

"Yes." Nausea overtook Maggie, who remembered that she'd had exactly the same reaction when she'd met Erin Dartford at the Lanvin show at London Fashion Week. She swallowed hard and tried to push the feeling away.

"Maggie, how lovely to see you again, and how good of you to come to my little soiree."

"Thank you for inviting us, Erin." Maggie knew she would have to shake the proffered hand, happy to skip the common gesture of a hug and an air-kiss. Fortunately, Erin didn't seem predisposed to such intimacy so Maggie lightly shook the dry talon, instantly desperate to wash off the contact.

And there was something in Erin's eyes too. Something that sent the nausea swelling inside Maggie again.

Erin's penetrating gaze moved onto Geoff. "You must be Maggie's husband. Geoff, I believe?"

"That's right. Pleased to meet you." Geoff happily shook Erin's hand with no negative reaction to it whatsoever.

Only one other couple lingered in the spacious hall. Surely more people would arrive soon. If not, they would be rattling around in this expansive place. Maggie considered simply going up to the other couple and introducing herself but an odd reluctance seized her, as though an invisible barrier surrounded them, as if Erin simply didn't want her guests to mingle. *What a stupid idea. This is a party, for heaven's sake. At parties people wander around chatting to each other.*

Despite her perfectly rational argument, Maggie stayed where she was. She took in the magnificent crystal chandelier with its numerous twinkling lights, the heavy emerald-green velvet drapes framing the massive windows on either side of the door, the pale lemon walls bedecked with paintings of ecclesiastical figures in scarlet and gold robes. They'd probably come with the place. The upkeep of such a home must cost a fortune. Geoff was right. Such wealth could surely not have been amassed in the short time Erin Dartford had been a force to be reckoned with in the fashion world. She must have come from money.

"Ah, here's your champagne. Please help yourselves and there are some little canapés as well. I don't want any of my guests fainting from hunger before dinner." Erin laughed and Geoff joined in. Maggie pretended but knew it was a halfhearted effort. She took a glass of champagne, drinking deeply.

Shoes scraped behind her and Erin's attention followed the sound. "Please excuse me, some other guests have arrived."

Maggie turned to see a face she recognized, although the poor girl didn't look at all well. "That's Nadine Cornwall. The model," she whispered to Geoff.

"I thought her face looked familiar."

"She looks positively green."

"I thought she looked pale and ethereal," Geoff said dramatically.

Maggie gave him a playful shove. "Don't be catty or I'll give you a saucer of milk."

"And you know I'll have you purring later."

Heat rose into Maggie's cheeks. In the ten years they'd been together, since shortly after her first husband's tragically early death from cancer, she'd never stopped feeling like an excited young girl in his arms. Even after all this time Geoff Lomax had the power to reduce her to a quivering pile of jelly. Although he had adored her and would have done anything for her, Liam had never managed to do that. Poor Liam.

"Hello, Maggie. You're looking grand, so you are."

Maggie gave a little cry and spun, nearly dropping her glass.

"What's the matter?" Geoff asked.

She whipped back round to face him. Her mouth was dry, her knees quivering. She was shaking from head to foot. "Who was that? Who spoke to me just now?"

"What? No one." Geoff apparently hadn't heard the voice and didn't have a clue what she was talking about.

"I heard him. I know I heard his voice."

"Who?"

"Liam."

Geoff raised his eyes to heaven. "Not that again. I thought we had gone past this. Liam's dead, Maggie."

"I heard him. I know it was him." Tears started to prickle the back of her eyes.

"Maybe you should go back to that shrink. We don't want you having those bloody nightmares again."

Maggie stared at him. Geoff seemed exasperated with her, as if he didn't believe her. *But I know what I heard. It can't have been in my head.* She thrust her half-drunk champagne at him. "I'll be back in a minute." Before he could ask where she was going, she was off, walking as quickly as she could out of the hall while trying not to attract any attention.

She stopped the waiter with the drinks tray. "Could you direct me to the bathroom, please?"

"Certainly, madam." He pointed down a long passageway.

She guessed that it must once have been a cloister but was now hung with tapestries. She scurried along, aware she was following a rapidly retreating Nadine Cornwall who'd beaten her to it. Damn! Maggie would either have to wait or try and find another bathroom. She decided on the latter. After all, in a house this size, there had to be more than one.

She passed four more closed doors and didn't try any of them, reasoning another bathroom was probably some distance away. At the end of the passage, she faced another closed door. She turned the handle.

The door opened into a library whose walls were lined with floor to ceiling shelves of books, mostly old and leather-bound. A large, gilt-framed mirror hung at one end of the room. In front of it were two large, winged, leather library chairs. They looked comfortable and inviting. She was tempted to sit for a while and gather her thoughts. She didn't really need a toilet, just somewhere she could reason out what had happened.

She made her way across the room and was about to sit when she caught sight of her reflection in the mirror. Her hair was a little disheveled. She lowered her eyes and popped open her small clutch to get a comb.

"Oh, to be sure you don't need to touch a hair of your pretty little head."

Maggie cried out again, saw her reflection in the mirror, and froze.

There, for one second, she'd seen two reflections. She was certain of it. One was hers.

The other, unmistakably, was Liam's.

She picked up her skirt, raced out of the room, and down the passage, ignoring Nadine. White-faced, Nadine seemed to stare straight through Maggie.

Her heart beating wildly, Maggie forced herself to slow down before she reached the hall where the couples still clung together. Another pair had joined them. Each couple seemed wrapped up in their own small world, oblivious to anyone else. Also preoccupied, she scooted back to Geoff, who wore a questioning look.

"We've got to get out of here. Now."

Geoff stared at her. "We can't leave, Maggie, we've only just got here. We haven't even had dinner yet. It would be the height of rudeness, and Erin Dartford is not the sort of woman I would want to get on the wrong side of."

"I don't care, Geoff, I really don't care. I've got to go."

"Look, I don't know what's going on but I'm telling you we can't leave. Hang on until after dinner and when a decent interval has elapsed, I promise you we'll make our excuses, but we can't go now. What's happened anyway? You're not usually like this."

"I don't usually see ghosts," she snapped.

"Ghosts?" Geoff laughed. "There's no such thing and you know it."

"Tell that to Liam."

"Oh, not that again. I told you—"

"I don't care what you told me. He's back. Liam's back and I know he's come for me."

Nick

"I hardly know the woman. Why on earth would she invite me to her house for dinner?" Nick Morton threw the invitation across the breakfast table where his wife, Deanna, picked it up and peered at it.

"You should get new glasses," Nick grunted.

Deanna pulled a face at him and held the card a little further away from her face. She read, "'Erin Dartford requests the pleasure of the company of Nick and Deanna Morton at her home, St. Saviour's Abbey, Little Hopton.' Nick, it's this Thursday. Oh, we must go. I mean, Erin Dartford of all people!"

"I haven't a clue why she would want us there and I have no intention of going," Nick grumbled.

"Surely you're not serious. Some people would kill for an invitation from her."

"Then let them fight over this one. Let them waste an evening of their lives and pretend to be Nick and Deanna Morton. I'm sure she wouldn't know the difference anyway. Hell, Deanna, I don't even remember where I met her!"

"Oh Nick, please! Look we hardly go anywhere these days as it is—"

"Rubbish! I took you to Saint-Tropez in the spring and Paris last autumn. Of course we go places."

"No, I don't mean holidays, I mean out for dinner. When was the last time we went to a party?"

"I hate parties."

"Oh Nick, please. Just this once. For my sake."

He hardly dared look at her. He knew she'd be doing that thing with her eyes again. And her nose. Yes, he was right, there was that little twitch and the "come-hither" look.

Damn her! She knew he couldn't resist her when she did that. *She knows me too well.* Still he did nothing to stem the wave of love—and lust—that surged over him. God alone knew why she loved him so much. His work left him stressed and moody much of the time yet she never complained. Not a day passed without him thanking whatever Supreme Being was out there for bringing her to him.

So she wanted to go to this party. She was right. He was so tied up at work, they rarely went out anywhere in the evenings, which had to be tough on her. She was twelve years younger than he and entitled to a bit of fun. And anyway, what would a couple of hours cost him? She would be bound to be grateful and when Deanna was grateful, Nick usually wound up being happy. Very happy indeed.

He swallowed a mouthful of strong coffee. "Oh, all right. We'll go. Tell her we accept. I've got to get to work. Advertising agencies don't run themselves, you know."

In the hall, Deanna handed him his laptop, and he bent to kiss her.

"Thank you, darling," she said, returning his kiss.

"For what?"

"Agreeing to go to Erin Dartford's party."

"What the hell? It's only for a few hours. And you're worth it." He imagined her in that gorgeous lacy black negligee he guessed she'd wear for him soon. Maybe even tonight. He pushed the thought aside. Reluctantly. "Got to get to work, angel." He kissed her again. "We'll continue this later. I should be home by seven. Meetings all day."

"They should give you a knighthood. Services to advertising. Arise Sir Nicholas Morton." She pretended to dub him on each shoulder.

Nick laughed as he opened the door. "Oh, I don't think so. It took them decades to give the first one out. Even now there aren't many. We're the bad boys, remember."

Deanna ran her tongue lasciviously over her lips. "Mmm. Well, tonight you can show me how bad."

"Don't start. Save it for later." He kissed her again, enjoying her warm body pressed against his. *God, I love this woman.*

London was frenetic as usual. Traffic backed up, even with the extortionate charges for driving in the inner city. *Bet most of this lot don't pay anyway.* He wondered, and not for the first time, why he didn't simply take the Tube. *Because it's cramped, dirty, smelly, and you can never get a seat, that's why.* Nick gritted his teeth and waited for the traffic to clear.

―――――

In his plush office on the twenty-second floor, he gazed out of the plate-glass windows over the rooftops of London. In the distance loomed the distinctive dome of St. Paul's Cathedral, while in the foreground, smaller office blocks jutted into the sky, many with rooftop gardens bathed in the sunlight of an already warm June day.

He was glad for the air-conditioning in his building. Out there, even the airless streets seemed to sweat. He had come a long way from those streets.

His drive and ambition had been the main reason Nestfield, Harvey, Morton had become one of the top advertising agencies in Europe. Next stop, the USA. He had done well … with Deanna at his side.

The clatter of heels dragged him back from his reverie. His PA had arrived with his coffee.

"Thanks, Sarah."

"I've brought your mail as well. Not much today. Seems to get less and less."

"No doubt that will be well and truly countered by the infinitely increasing volume of emails that come bouncing into our inboxes."

Sarah grimaced. "At least our new system seems to be working. They come straight to me and I filter out the crap before forwarding onto you."

"Well, I'd better get to it. Find out what is so important it can't be dealt with by the best PA in London."

"Flatterer."

Nick smiled at her. He wasn't kidding. She very probably *was* the best PA in London. She certainly took a lot of the heat off him. His inbox had overflowed with emails every day, but now Sarah dealt with them. The only ones he received were forwarded by her to a new email account he had opened, the details of which were known only to the two of them. And that was only one of her many innovations designed to make his life run more smoothly. After his first PA died so tragically six years ago, Sarah joined him and he had wondered whether to persuade her to fill both vacancies left by Laura's death—the one in his office and the one in his bed—but she made it abundantly clear early on that she was happily tied to a longstanding girlfriend. "Sorry Nick, no hard feelings, but you could never be my type, if you see what I mean." They had laughed about that many times since. Deanna had joined the company as his business partner's PA and that was it. One look at her and his philandering days were over.

"Your coffee's getting cold," Sarah said.

Nick drained his cup. "My first appointment is at ten, isn't it?"

"Yes. Charlie Davidson from Talbot Holdings. And you have lunch with Steve Tarleton and Jay van Zandt."

He rolled his eyes. "No doubt Jay will want to tell me all about his latest sports car, and Steve will regale me with tales of his latest conquest."

"Lamborghini."

"What?"

"Jay van Zandt's new car is a Lamborghini. I asked his PA and there's a leaflet about it with your mail, so you can sound as if you know what you're talking about."

"You *are* the best PA in London. Thank you." He leaned back in his chair and interlocked his fingers behind his head. "You know, I love and hate this business. The bit I hate is the arse kissing I have to do before the likes of prats like Jay van Zandt."

"His account's worth eight million to the agency."

"I know. That's the bit I love. The billings. The money. And I especially like taking Jay van Zandt's money. God, that man's a total prick."

She laughed and left the office, closing the door behind her.

He booted up his computer and logged onto his email account. Fifteen messages to deal with. Not bad. Before Sarah's new system, he'd have received at least fifty overnight. He scanned down them quickly. Most were providing management information. A couple of them were invitations to appear at prestigious events. The BBC wanted him to appear in a political debate show.

Then he came to one whose subject line really caught his eye.

John Stone.

Nick hadn't heard that name in seven years. Not since …

It couldn't be the same one. The John Stone he knew was dead. Long dead and buried.

Nick opened the email and stared at it.

"Remember me? It's been a long time but I remember you, Nick Morton, and I remember what you did. To me. To my family. Now it's your turn to pay."

With trembling hands, Nick picked up his phone.

"Sarah. Get in here. Now," he barked and a second later she was at his desk.

"Where the hell did this come from? And why did you send it to me?"

Sarah frowned and came around to his side of the desk. Peering over his shoulder, she read the email.

"Well?"

"Nick, I'm sorry, but I've never seen that before in my life. If you look, all the emails I send you are forwarded. This one has come directly from the sender. Except … well …"

"Except what?"

"See for yourself. There is no sender. The box saying who it's from is blank."

Nick looked closer. She was right. The message was anonymous. He hit 'Reply' but it wouldn't work. An error message flashed up each time he tried it.

"Try clicking the 'Show details' tab. That usually gives you an email address for the sender," she said.

He did so. The sender box was empty.

"Well, I've never seen that before. Do you want me to get our IT guys on it?"

"Yes, Sarah. I think that would be a good idea. Right away please, and sorry for bawling you out like that."

"No problem. Understandable really. It's a bit unnerving getting an email like that, especially when you can't even trace where it's come from."

"How in hell did this person get hold of this address?"

"Beats me. Do you want to get a new one?" Nick hesitated, but only for an instant. That email had really disturbed him. He didn't want any more. "Yes. I'll set one up on Gmail and let you have the details."

Ten minutes later he had a new email account and was about to let Sarah have the details when a message dropped into his box. Probably spam, or another one of those interminable "welcome" messages.

The subject line was blank. He clicked onto it and caught his breath.

"It's me again. John Stone. You don't get rid of me that easily and nor do you push your guilt aside either. It's your time to pay for what you did. There's no escape."

By nine forty-five, Nick had opened six new email addresses with six different providers and each time, before he could let Sarah know the details, up came the same message. It was no use. He might as well keep the original one. On the way out to his meeting, he told her what had happened.

"This is all very odd," she said. "I'll talk to the head of IT and see if he has any ideas how to stop it."

Thanking her, he went out to the elevator.

———

He didn't tell Deanna what had happened. In fact, in all the years they had been together, as far as he could remember, John Stone's name had never been mentioned. There had been no need. Deanna wouldn't have had a clue who he was anyway. But as he lay in bed next to his wife, his mind drifted back.

Nine years ago, he had started an affair with his PA, Laura Stone, and she had blurted it all out to her husband one night in the middle of a row. Nick remembered what had happened all too clearly. She had turned up on his doorstep in the middle of a torrential thunderstorm, a suitcase in one hand and her eight-year-old son clinging onto the other.

"I've left him, Nick. I've told him it's over and that you and I are together."

He remembered staring at them in disbelief for a few seconds, oblivious to the fact that they were soaked to the skin, and the boy was shivering.

"Nick. Please let us in."

Feeling trapped, he had stood to one side, without a word, his thoughts jumbled. He hadn't planned for this at all. Laura was a pretty woman with a great pair of tits, but she wasn't his idea of a life partner. Theirs was a casual, sex-centered relationship. He would feel horny, and she would come into his office, lock the door, and strip. The sex was hot, satisfying, simple, no-strings shagging. No one was to know. No one was to get hurt.

Except of course, someone had. Well, her husband had anyway. After that night, she moved in, and his bachelor existence had been overtaken by kids' train sets, computer games, children's TV ... and John Stone.

And Nick hadn't loved her. Not then. Not at any time. He liked the sex and played trains with the boy. Some nights he stayed away altogether and enjoyed some other woman's warm bed. He never explained his absences to her questioning eyes, and he had no conscience about it. Not for one second.

Then he met John Stone, clearly a broken man. Laura had told Nick that her husband was a successful accountant but the shambling wreck who stood before him, dropping off his son after a weekend visit, looked more like a tramp. John Stone hadn't shaved for at least a week. His clothes were stained and unwashed. A heavy and shocking odor of alcohol had emanated from him.

Worse, his young son, Andy, wrenched his hand out of his father's and grabbed hold of Nick's, squeezing it tightly as if scared he might have to go back to his father.

Stone radiated pain, but what could Nick have said? Stone was an unfit father and until he cleaned himself up—in more ways than one—he wouldn't be able to see Andy alone, if at all. Loser.

As far as Nick knew, that had been the last time Stone saw his son, but that hadn't been the last time Nick saw Stone. Laura persuaded Nick to go with her to Stone's small rented apartment one evening while her parents babysat for Andy. At the time, John and Laura had been separated for over a year. Stone had lost his job six months earlier because of his drinking. Nick also guessed that John would have taken Laura back if she would go. Maybe she would, if he hadn't been so far down the road of self-destruction. She surely couldn't be happy living with a man who showed her no more than a passing casual consideration and then only after a night of sex.

They'd arrived at a rundown council-owned housing estate in a rough part of town, Gypsy Farm. Even the police shuddered when they got a call to investigate an incident there. As Nick had locked the car, he'd been aware of sullen eyes staring at him from street corners and, as they made their way to the battered front door, he'd seen a discarded hypodermic casually tossed onto a meager stretch of grass. His nerve endings twitched with revulsion.

John had taken a good five minutes to open the door, and he'd been drunk. Laura's hand had flown to cover her nose, while Nick had recoiled from the stench of unwashed body, stale urine, and moldy food. As they followed him through the apartment, Nick saw that in the kitchen was a heap of filthy, encrusted dishes, piled in the sink. An overflowing bin had reeked in the corner and (mostly) empty food cartons had been tossed casually on the work surfaces. The cooker had been covered in grease, and an ancient frying pan held evidence of fry-ups stuck to its bottom. The living room had been littered with old newspapers and dirty clothes. The TV had been smashed to pieces, and empty vodka bottles were everywhere.

"Oh my God, John, what sort of mess have you got yourself into?" Laura had tried to find somewhere to sit but couldn't. Nick had wondered if they'd catch something nasty.

John had been so drunk he could barely speak. His hair had grown long, thin, and unkempt. His skin had a yellowish pallor, as did his eyes. He'd seemed to have simply given up and was waiting for the end. Perhaps he'd even hasten it.

Maybe I should pity him. After all, from his angle I stole his wife and child. But I'm not responsible for all this shit. He could have rebuilt his life. He chose not to. Nick had no time for "losers" as he called them. And, to him, John had defined loser.

John had managed to croak out a response ... directed at Nick. Though he'd been barely audible, Nick hadn't missed the venom behind the words. "You took my Laura. You poisoned my son against me. You left me with nothing. *Nothing.* I will never forget that. To my dying day. From beyond the grave. I *curse* you, Morton." Nick had been chilled by the words, by the intensity.

A week later John Stone died, and three months after that, Laura came off the road and crashed her car into a tree, killing herself and her son outright. No other vehicle had been involved, and the car was in perfect working order. The evidence pointed to her driving without due care and attention, distracted, perhaps by her son, or her other woes. Nick knew she'd blamed herself for John's decline and death and had been behaving strangely. He had caught her one day with a load of pills in her hand, apparently about to swallow them all. The next day, she'd told him she didn't love him anymore.

"I always loved John. Always. I should never have left him for you."

He'd dropped any pretense he'd cared. "You're right. You shouldn't have. Why did you?"

"Because I thought I was in love with you, you bastard!"

"It was sex, Laura. I enjoyed having sex with you. It relieved my frustrations. I thought you knew that."

She had flown at him. He still had a small scar on his jaw where her long nails lacerated him. She screamed and cursed him, grabbed her terrified son and bundled him into her car, driving off at such a high speed that the tires squealed.

The police had knocked on his door two hours later. Evidently she had been driving to her sister-in-law's ten miles away, even though Chloe was in Australia and hadn't even been able to get back until after

Laura's funeral. Nick had never met her, even though she and Laura had been close.

Now, in his bed, he tossed and turned, unable to find sleep. Beside him Deanna slept on, still dressed in the lacy black negligee he had enjoyed negotiating his way around earlier. She'd shown her gratitude with her usual enthusiasm and inventiveness, but even her best efforts couldn't stop him from worrying about those emails.

Who had sent them and what did they want?

Nadine

Nadine felt Paul's eyes burning into her, and she couldn't look at him. He seemed to want an explanation for her protracted absence, but what could she tell him? After she had shot out of that bathroom, she had leaned, panting against the wall, trying to calm herself, desperately telling herself that she had imagined that voice. Yet Julie's Lancashire accent was so distinctive. As long as she lived, Nadine knew she would never forget it or the events of that awful night. The last night she had seen Julie alive.

How could she explain the mist that had descended in that tapestry-walled passageway, or the shapes that started to emerge? How could she explain the awful smell of burning and the lost minutes when she must have fainted?

She needed to eat something. That was all.

But … She had starved herself many times before and never once hallucinated. She looked around at the other couples. This was certainly a strange dinner party. Apart from chatting to Erin, no one seemed to be mingling. The only other person in the room she recognized was Maggie O'Donnell, that writer whose books were virtually the only ones she read, and then only on long plane journeys. From time to time, she caught furtive glances from another guest, and she began to realize that she wasn't the only one who felt uneasy tonight.

"Come on, Nadine, snap out of it. Try some of these hors d'oeuvres. I don't know what's in them, but they are very tasty." Paul handed her a tiny canapé.

She took a small bite and grimaced. "Oh God, Paul, it's vile. It's so bitter. What the hell has she put in here?"

"What are you talking about? I've had one. They're gorgeous. A kind of curried chicken."

She thrust it back at him. "Whatever that is, it is not curried chicken."

His quizzical expression remained until he sniffed at and popped the offending morsel in his mouth. "Exactly the same as the one I had. Delicious," he said, swallowing and wiping his hands on a small linen napkin handed to him by a passing waiter. "Honestly, Nadine, I think you're losing it today."

She glared at him, opened her mouth to say something cutting but decided against it. Not here. Not now.

"This is weird," she said, watching Erin speak to one of the two liveried waiters. "Have you wondered what we are all doing here? I mean, there's no atmosphere, apart from a little piped Muzak in the background. No one is mingling, and our hostess doesn't seem inclined to encourage it anyway. Everyone looks wary."

"Perhaps they're all waiting for someone to make the first move. Maybe our Miss Dartford isn't the hostess type. Maybe she invites a collection of people and sits back to watch what happens. Who knows? Come on, I am much more interested in what happened to you while you were away all that time. Did you meet the resident ghost?"

"Paul, how long have we been together? As a couple, I mean."

"About eighteen months. Why?"

"And in that time, have you ever known me to behave in an irrational way?"

He laughed. "Do you really want me to answer that one?"

"No, I'm being serious. I know I get a bit premenstrual sometimes—"

"Not to mention the stressing out when your hair won't sit right or your latest designer dress doesn't hang the way you think it should."

"You know what I'm getting at. I'm not one to imagine voices in my head or see … Oh, I don't know what I saw. But something in this house doesn't feel right and something about our hostess doesn't gel either."

"Oh come on, Nadine." He sounded exasperated.

She was about to tell him to forget it when Erin Dartford's shrill voice called above the muted conversation. "Ladies and gentlemen. Dinner is served, if you would all like to follow me."

The four couples filed in two by two in total silence. It's almost like going to a funeral, Nadine thought. But why? She caught Maggie O'Donnell's eye fleetingly before the writer looked away, apparently searching for her name card on the table.

"Please be seated, everyone." Again Nadine noticed how Erin's smile never moved beyond her slightly upturned lips. Her eyes were everywhere, not missing one single move.

Nadine shivered and found her place, between Maggie's husband and another man she didn't know. In front of her was her favorite starter, Parma ham wrapped around slices of melon and chunks of fresh peach. She saw that, in front of each guest was a different dish and, by their reactions, each person was being served their favorite cold starter. Opposite her, sitting between Maggie and a very pretty blonde woman, Paul caught her eye and pointed at his plate of caviar and smoked salmon. His favorite. He smiled and nodded at her dish. Nadine managed to return his smile but the fear that had been haunting her since they'd arrived knotted itself tighter in her stomach.

She turned to Maggie's husband and was about to ask him how he reckoned Erin could have known so much about her guests' tastes in food, when their hostess tapped her wine glass.

"Ladies and gentlemen, I hope you enjoy your meal. However, as is the way with these things, I am quite sure some of you will enjoy it more than others."

"What a curious thing to say." Nadine realized she had spoken out loud. Neither of her neighbors seemed to have noticed but, judging by the way Paul was staring at her as she raised her fork to her mouth, it appeared he had. He wore a triumphant expression and she didn't know why.

She stuck her fork into a chunk of juicy peach and put it into her mouth.

Her world exploded.

Gary

When he woke up to the sound of an overenthusiastic radio DJ, he figured he had imagined the voice in the bathroom. After all, he had been half-asleep and unnerved by the nightmare.

"You look like you're ready to go to bed, not get up from it," Melissa said as she hooked up her bra. Looking at her still-perfect breasts restricted by the tight black lingerie, Gary's erection rose. *Down boy. You've got to go to work, remember.*

With a sigh, he swung his long legs over the side of the bed and stood.

Melissa glanced at his midriff, then quickly turned away. It wasn't the first time. His heart sank. He knew there was something wrong with their marriage but he had no idea what it was or what he could do about it. When he thought about it, he couldn't even pinpoint when things had started to change. Maybe their inability to have children bothered her, although she'd never mentioned that. He had come home early last week and found her in tears, but when he had tried to comfort her, she'd stiffened at his touch. She had insisted it was hormonal, saying, "I always get a bit weepy around my time of the month." He had almost believed her, except she had used the same excuse two weeks earlier.

No, Melissa was clearly upset about something, and Gary resolved to get to the bottom of it. Maybe Erin's party would help cheer her up a bit. She could have a few drinks, relax a little. Then she might tell him what was wrong, and they could start putting it right.

"I should be home by six," he said, trying to keep it light.

"OK," Melissa said, as if only half-listening while she brushed her hair and studied her reflection in the mirror.

He watched her in silence. She seemed oblivious to his presence. He didn't tell her what the meeting was about, that it was probably the most important in his career so far.

She didn't seem to care, so what was the point?

His earlier despondency evaporated with the events of the day, and he decided to tell her his good news in the car as they drove to Erin's party. "The meeting went really well with the CEO. It looks like they'll offer me a directorship at last. It'll mean one hell of a pay rise and I'll have to travel more, but we'll be able to afford that detached cottage in the country you always wanted." He glanced over at Melissa in the passenger seat.

She smiled at him. But he could swear she only seemed to half-hear him, as if a part of her simply wasn't there. As always, though, she had risen to the occasion. Her long hair was swept up on her head, and her ears glittered with the diamond drop earrings he had bought her for her last birthday. At her throat hung a matching necklace. It had cost a packet but she was worth every penny to him. If only he could make their marriage work again.

Her dress too was costly, but she hadn't had to pay for it. She had told him that Erin had given it to her as a "thank you" for the excellent job she was doing as her PA. Gary couldn't remember the name of the designer but the dress could have been made for her. It sheathed her body in rich red silk from her shoulders to her ankles and clung in all the right places. "You could have been a model," he said, not for the first time.

And not for the first time, Melissa laughed at the suggestion. "Oh no, not me, I like pie too much."

At least *that* sounded like the Melissa he knew and loved. Gary stopped the Range Rover in front of the ornate gates, which were already starting to swing open.

"This puts a different take on the country pile, doesn't it? It's not everyone who can afford their own abbey. Where has she got her money from, anyway?"

"She works incredibly hard and she's very well thought of in the business. And there are all the commissioned features. They pay megabucks."

"And she's earned enough in the past couple of years to afford this? I'm definitely in the wrong business."

They drew up to the stone steps and, once out of the car, ascended to the top.

"Do you suppose we just walk in?" Gary asked.

"She's quite informal. I'm sure that will be fine. Why leave the door open if you don't expect your guests to wander in?"

A striking figure in black descended on them. "Melissa, darling! And you've brought your lovely husband with you. Excellent. Hello, Gary. I'm Erin Dartford. Welcome to the Hallowed Hall. Oh yes, Melissa, I know what everyone calls it!" She laughed but Gary was struck by how hollow it sounded. How forced.

He pushed the thought away and took her scarlet-nailed hand. It felt like parchment. "Pleased to meet you," he managed through gritted teeth. He dredged up a smile and caught her scrutinizing him in a way that made him want to bolt, as if she was invading his mind, searching around for something. The expression was fleeting, but Gary was left with the sense she had got what she was looking for. That bothered him.

"A waiter will be around shortly with champagne and please help yourself to canapés." Erin was saying all the right things and, beside him, Melissa was behaving normally. She seemed totally at ease in Erin's company.

"Are we too early?" He nodded over at the empty vastness of the entrance hall. Even speaking quietly, his voice echoed and bounced off the marble pillars.

"We are quite a select little gathering this evening," Erin said. "I much prefer intimate dinner parties to large crowds, don't you? It means I can talk to everyone and won't skip anyone." She peered over his shoulder. "Oh, please excuse me. I see someone else has arrived."

Erin hurried off, and Gary took two glasses of champagne off the tray held by the expressionless waiter, handing one to Melissa. "So that's the great Erin Dartford. Strange old bird, isn't she?"

Melissa looked horrified. "Gary, please. Be careful what you say. She'll hear you."

He took a healthy slug of his drink. "At least she knows a decent champagne when she sees one. OK, if she's not going to introduce us, let's do it for ourselves. Come on." He took her hand to lead her toward the couple who had just arrived.

"What are you doing? Stop it!" Melissa pulled her hand away.

"What? This is a party. I'm going to *party*. That means meeting the other guests."

"No, Gary."

"What do you mean 'no, Gary'?"

"I think we should wait a bit, that's all. Let's settle into our surroundings, drink our champagne, and—"

"Settle into our surroundings? Melissa, we're not moving house, we're at a party. At a party, people talk to each other."

"And at a party, the guests should take their lead from the hostess. Erin will decide when we should mingle."

Gary stared at her. "What's got into you all of a sudden? I've never known you behave like this before."

"She's my boss, Gary, I don't want to get anything wrong. She's normally very easygoing as you can see, but I wouldn't want to upset her."

Personally, he thought his brief encounter with Erin had been anything but easygoing. He'd felt mentally assaulted by her, but it was best to keep quiet about that. It might get him into dangerous waters. "OK, Mel, if you say so. But it's a very strange party where the guests keep themselves firmly to themselves and don't get together."

"Oh, I expect it will be different when everyone's here."

"How many are due to come? I'm assuming you sent out the invitations."

Melissa sipped her champagne, then shook her head. "Not this time. Erin did it all herself."

Gary was attracted by a movement at the door. "There's two more at any rate. I know that woman from somewhere."

"That's the model, Nadine Cornwall."

"Do you know any of the others?"

Melissa shook her head again. "I'm not sure but I think the woman over there in green is a writer. She looks a little familiar, and I think we may have seen her at one of the catwalk shows, but I can't remember her name. As for the others … No, I don't know them."

Another couple arrived, so the party numbered eight guests. The minutes ticked by and Gary helped himself to more champagne. Still, no one seemed inclined to get to know their fellow guests. Each couple stood, almost like sentries stationed at each corner of the room. Gary had even lost the will to be the first to initiate contact. Surely Erin would get things started soon.

"OK, before this party starts to heat up or at least develop some kind of atmosphere, I'm off to the gents. That champagne has gone straight through me. Grab me another, will you, babe?"

Melissa nodded and Gary headed for an open door leading to a long passageway. He had seen two women emerge from there, so he assumed that must be the way to the bathroom. He passed by the model and could see she was visibly shaking. *Drugs probably.*

He located the bathroom, locked the door behind him and took care of business. When he washed his hands, he heard it again.

"Mummy. Help me! I'm lost."

A chill swept through him. His reflection was white-faced, drained.

A shadow passed behind him, and he froze. Swallowing, he turned slowly. Nothing.

He regarded the mirror again and caught sight of a ghostly image flickering on and off in an instant.

But that instant was enough for Gary to recognize someone he hadn't seen for ten years.

Patrick Morgan.

"Whatever's the matter, Gary? You're trembling."

She was right. His hands were shaking so hard he couldn't take the glass from her. "I don't know, Mel, I've just seen something impossible. Heard something impossible. I think we need to go. Now, preferably."

"I can't go now, Gary! She's my boss."

He stared at her. She was right. He was being unreasonable. Of course they couldn't leave. Out of the corner of his eye, he caught sight of another couple, that writer and her husband. She was agitated and kept glancing over at the door, while it was clear that he had no intention of moving, preferring to help himself to another glass of champagne. He'd swear they were having a similar conversation.

"Ladies and gentlemen. Dinner is served if you would all like to follow me."

Melissa took Gary's arm but not before he had seen her take a deep breath … Why?

They followed Nadine and her partner into the dining room. He found his place card where his favorite starter, dressed crab, awaited him. He glanced at Melissa, seated at the opposite side of the table. She had Greek salad, the appetizer she always ordered if it was on the menu. She had an apprehensive expression in her eyes but, as she caught him looking at her, it was quickly replaced by a smile. She nodded toward the crab. Still unnerved by his experience in the bathroom, he managed a weak returning smile and sat. He saw her exchange a few brief words with the man sitting next to her. The writer's husband, who nodded and smiled.

Erin gave a little speech of welcome. Despite her kind words, he was overtaken by a wave of revulsion against this woman. But why? He'd never met her before.

Trying to shrug it off, he picked up his fork and dug into the crab. He took a bite and …

… He was on a deserted street on a freezing January night.

Maggie

"I'm sorry, Maggie, but you can't seriously expect me to believe that Liam's ghost somehow hitched a ride with us over here to a place he has never been to before and materialized in a library mirror. I mean, come on, can't you see how ridiculous this all is?"

She hesitated. Put like that, of course it was. "But I know what I saw and what I heard. I would know Liam's face and voice anywhere. I *was* married to him for nine years."

"Yes, nearly as long as you've been married to me. You know, it's rather strange, Maggie. You've carried this guilt around with you all these years and yet within a few months of your husband's death, you were virtually galloping up the aisle with me."

Maggie glared at him. "What do you mean by that? I loved Liam. I loved him and I had to watch him die."

"But that's not strictly true, is it? You *weren't* there when he died. You were sipping cocktails in the bar at the Chateau Marmont hotel in Beverly Hills with your lover when Liam O'Donnell breathed his last, weren't you?"

"Keep your voice down, Geoff. We don't want everyone to hear our business."

"No? Well I shouldn't think your first husband liked it a whole lot when you deserted him in the last week of his life so that you could swan off to LA and sign a film contract. I'm pretty sure that he was pissed off by that. I know I would have been."

She dropped her voice to a furious stage whisper. "Liam knew why I had to go. He supported my decision."

Geoff snorted. "You told me yourself he begged you not to put him in a nursing home. Good God, woman, what would it have cost you to wait another week? The film company would have understood in the circumstances."

"I couldn't take the risk. It was my first chance. My big breakthrough. My first novel had been picked up by a tiny publisher. Whoever would have thought that a major Hollywood director would want to film it?"

Maggie saw a strange look in Geoff's eyes that she couldn't read. He paused before he spoke. And when he did, his voice was icy. "So you let him die alone in agony in a nursing home among strangers. I hope it was worth it, Maggie. I really do."

"Ladies and gentlemen. Dinner is served if you would all like to follow me."

She and Geoff walked in silence out of the hall following another couple. Maggie's mind was racing. Why was Geoff so upset with her? After all, Liam was nothing to him. Why wouldn't he at least acknowledge that something very real and frightening had happened to her in this house?

He was usually so understanding when she had one of those dreadful recurring nightmares. Even after all this time, she recoiled from the image that had plagued her night after night.

Liam's hand reaching out to her. Bony and covered with maggots.

In the dining room, she located her place next to a man she thought was Nadine Cornwall's husband or partner. Maggie looked diagonally across at the model and met her glance before she turned away. But in that instant, Maggie saw that Nadine was scared stiff. She looked exactly how Maggie felt, an unwanted connection.

She glanced down at her plate. How could Erin possibly know that beef carpaccio was her favorite cold starter? She looked around the table. Everyone appeared to have a different dish and, judging by their expressions, Erin had got it right every time. Her fellow guests were staring in wonder at their favorite food. Even Geoff seemed to have cheered up at the sight of a mouthwatering avocado and prawn salad.

Maggie looked up toward the head of the table where their hostess seemed to be waiting for something, although she couldn't think what, as all the guests were seated. The conversation was muted and there were even the stirrings of a little mingling although she herself was far too wound up to join in.

She eyed Erin, riveted by her body language. Their hostess was a strange one, without a doubt. Glossy black hair framed her face in such a way that it reminded her of an old photograph of the twenties actress Louise Brooks. Erin even had the slash of crimson lipstick to complete the effect. Her long, black dress was interwoven with glittery threads. Her neck was unadorned with any jewelry, as were her ears, but her long, claw-like fingers were festooned with rings, including one massive ruby. *Surely it can't be real. It would cost a fortune.*

The overall effect was of a striking woman who seemed to give off some kind of aura. Erin Dartford could step into any room, stop the conversation, and turn heads. Not because she was beautiful. She wasn't. But because she was an irresistible force.

Who was she? A little more than two years ago Maggie had never heard of Erin Dartford and, as far as she knew, neither had anyone in the fashion industry. Then, suddenly, there she was, writing features on leading designers and rapidly acquiring a reputation as a career maker-or-breaker in the refined world of haute couture. Models, designers, all fell at her feet to worship at the altar of Erin, but no one really knew how she'd ascended.

Maggie was barely aware of Erin's welcoming speech but instead was transfixed by her hostess's eyes. Piercingly blue, like glittering sapphires, they seemed to cut through to the soul of everyone sitting around that table.

A cool draft passed over Maggie along with the scent of a long-forgotten aftershave. Hugo Boss.

Her breath stopped. Geoff never wore it, but Liam had.

Glancing over at Geoff, she saw him exchange a few brief words with a female guest. She glanced at Nadine's partner. Maybe he was wearing the fragrance, but oddly, it had only wafted over to her for an instant. But he had to be the source.

For whatever reason, she was imagining all sorts of crazy things. Like the thought that this delicious-looking beef carpaccio would taste bitter when she started to eat it. *I need to see that psychiatrist again.*

Everyone else had picked up their forks or spoons, so she selected the outermost cutlery. She cut off a morsel of the carpaccio and raised it to her mouth.

And her world changed forever.

Nick

"I thought our house was big but if we lived in this one we could go a week without seeing each other." Nick stood on the driveway and took in the illuminated abbey.

Deanna slid her hand into his. "We already go a week without seeing one another."

"Don't start that again." He squeezed her hand. "I brought you here, didn't I?"

"You did. I can't deny that. A little unwillingly though. You've been even grumpier than usual these past few days. Goodness knows why because you won't confide in me."

"Just work, angel, that's all. Just work." But he knew it wasn't and he rather guessed she did too.

"You must be Nick Morton and this is your lovely wife Deanna." A bony, ringed hand edged with scarlet nails, presented itself.

He took it, shaking it quickly and, for some reason, hating the experience. She had the oddest skin. Papery. He reached for the handkerchief in his pocket and wiped his hand as surreptitiously as he could.

"Where have we met, Erin?" he asked her. "I've been trying to remember."

"The Campaign Awards last year, I believe. I was a guest of Vernon Ritter."

"BBH?" He named a famous ad agency.

Erin paused for a second. "Yes, that's right. BBH. Do help yourselves to champagne. We shall be going into dinner shortly as we're all here. I do hope you're hungry. We have all your favorites."

"Would you introduce us to your other guests? We don't know anyone here."

"Oh, I'm sure you'll get to know each other. In time." With that, Erin slid away from them, leaving the room. Her guests remained rigidly in each of the four corners of the vast hall, speaking in hushed whispers that echoed off the stone to creepy effect.

"What a strange party," Nick said. "Still I suppose it beats having to make small talk with people you couldn't care less about."

"Oh, Nick." Deanna gave him an affectionate shove. "You're such an antisocial pig at times. Have a drink. Maybe you'll relax a little."

He accepted the glass from Deanna and glanced around the room. "She's got some expensive stuff here. Fancy a closer look at the sculptures? There's a pair of nice bronzes over there by the door."

"That's a bit cheeky, isn't it? Inspecting your hostess's things without being invited to do so."

"It's also a bit cheeky bringing a guest here on false pretenses."

Deanna looked at him questioningly. Moving aside a large rose bowl filled with heavily scented orange blooms, he set down his glass on a nearby marble table with a click. "She said she was a guest of Vernon Ritter at last year's Campaign Awards. I asked her if she meant Vernon Ritter from BBH and she said it was."

"So?"

"Vernon Ritter doesn't work for BBH and never has. I've known Vern for years. He works for WPP. She lied, Deanna. If I had met her at the Campaign Awards I would have remembered. She's not exactly easy to forget, is she? I mean, look at her, she's pretty distinctive."

Deanna looked at Erin, who had reentered the room and cleared her throat, possibly in advance of making an announcement.

"Maybe she had her hair done differently and maybe she got the name of the agency wrong."

"And maybe she was never there in the first place."

"Oh Nick, you're so suspicious. You think everyone's got an ulterior motive for everything."

"With what's been happening to me these past few days, I'd be suspicious of my own mother if she was still alive."

"What *has* been happening, Nick? Won't you tell me?"

He hesitated, then shook his head. *Best you don't know. What you don't know can't hurt you.*

"Ladies and gentlemen. Dinner is served if you would all like to follow me."

Nick smiled at Deanna and took her hand, slipping it over his arm. "Come on, let's see what she's laid on for us. Whatever she's up to, we can at least get a free dinner out of it."

He glanced at her, noting an odd expression on her face, almost secretive, as if she knew something he didn't. Nick couldn't imagine what it was. She didn't know anything about the emails he had been getting. One or two a day since Monday, always arriving directly to his inbox and untraceable. IT seemed powerless to either stop them or find their point of origin. He had deleted the last two without reading them.

"*That was a silly thing to do, Nick. And it won't prevent the inevitable.*"

"What?" Nick shot a look behind him. No one there. They were bringing up the rear.

Deanna tugged at his sleeve. "What's the matter now?"

"Nothing. I thought I heard someone speak, that's all."

Again that strange look. He was about to question her about it when they arrived at the dinner table and he saw a plate of *antipasto misto*, his favorite cold starter. Deanna had got a bowl of gazpacho, which was what she would have chosen for herself.

Astonishing. A woman they'd never met had invited them to a select dinner party. She'd gone to the trouble of discovering their favorite cold appetizers … and everyone else's, judging by the pleased, surprised reactions around the table.

What was going on here?

Nick shook his head and sat down. No doubt answers would be forthcoming later. Meanwhile, the *antipasto* looked delicious. He forked a slice of salami into his mouth …

… and found himself in a chilly, rundown apartment.

Nadine

"*You remember me, don't you?*"

Nadine didn't dare open her eyes, but she knew where she was. She was no longer at Erin Dartford's dinner table.

She could smell a scent she hadn't come across for years. A fake jasmine. Not a perfume, an aerosol air freshener, the sort Julie used to buy. Nadine had always hated it. It smelled cheap and common, but years ago, cheap and common was all she could afford.

But she'd always been sure she was destined for a better life.

"*You always said you were going to be a top model. That you were going to topple Kate Moss from her throne. You were going to wear all those fancy clothes and have Donatella Versace and Stella McCartney on your speed dial.*"

Afraid of what she might see, Nadine still didn't open her eyes, terrified of what she might have to confront. A shaky but defiant voice spoke … hers. "I did get somewhere. I got to the top."

A tinny laugh echoed around her. "*Maybe, Nadine, maybe. But at what cost?*"

"Who *are* you?"

"*You know who I am. Why don't you open your eyes? I'm right here, Nadine. Right where you left me.*"

The stink of ashes and smoke clogged her lungs. Nadine's eyes shot open. Standing directly in front of her was the familiar freckled face of her oldest friend, Julie, so close that if Nadine reached out her hand, they'd touch.

But Julie wasn't actually standing on the floor. She was hovering a few inches above it. Nadine gasped. The reek was much closer; smoke seeped under a closed door at the end of the hall.

She realized where she was. She was back in their flat, the one they'd shared five years before. And if she was to open that door, she'd see fire. The curtains would be flaming, the inferno caused by the candles they'd lit to celebrate Nadine's first modeling contract.

But this was all wrong. It couldn't be happening. Julie was dead. She'd died in the fire.

And I am not here. I am sitting around a dinner table with some people I have never met before.

"You remember that night, don't you, Nadine? You remember how you came home, so proud of yourself, brandishing two bottles of Cava and ready to celebrate. You remember lighting your scented candles. I told you not to put them so close to the curtains but you told me they were safe."

"You moved them. You must have moved them. They *were* safe."

Julie shook her head. *"I went to change the CD and I heard a noise. When I turned, the curtains had shot up in flames. I screamed but you never heard me."*

"Why didn't you get out? You could have got to the door in time."

"I panicked and caught my foot in the rug. I fell. Hard enough and awkwardly enough to break my ankle. I grabbed the bookcase as I fell and it toppled onto my leg. It was too heavy for me to shift and I was pinned down. In agony. I screamed your name but you didn't come."

"I never heard you. Not until it was too late." Nadine was sobbing. But Julie hadn't finished with her yet.

The image before her changed. Nadine was in their shabby, little kitchen, a new bottle of Cava in her hand. She stared down at it. In the distance, a muffled cry. Julie was calling her. She was in trouble. Maybe this time she could save her. Maybe this time it would be all right. She'd been given a second chance. *Thank you merciful Lord. Thank you.*

She dropped the bottle, hearing it smash on the floor as she raced out of the kitchen. Seeing the smoke seeping under the door, she grabbed the handle. Burning hot. She immediately snatched her hand away.

Her brain racing, she dived back into the kitchen and grabbed a towel. Wrapping it around her hand, she tugged at the handle and opened the door into a rapidly escalating conflagration. Lying on the floor, on the far side of the room, a sobbing Julie was reaching out to her. "Help me, Nadine. *Please* save me. I can't move!"

The fire raged, snarling through the cheap furnishings, which produced clouds of toxic smoke, choking Nadine's lungs. Coughing, her eyes were watering while Julie was screaming, "*Get me out get me out.*"

The window smashed, spraying shards of glass everywhere. The rush of oxygen fed the flames so they raged more fiercely.

Julie's screams tore through her. *It's all happening again. Just like before.*

And like before, Nadine hesitated. If she acted now, she might get her friend out. But she could get burned herself, destroying her career before it had even started. No one would ever hear of Nadine Cornwall. She would be horribly disfigured. Hell, even now as she choked on the smoke, she could barely see Julie, her hair singeing, her screams ever more terrible as the flames started to lick at her feet.

The screams stopped. Too late.

Nadine had missed her chance.

"*I curse you, Nadine Cornwall. I curse you to burn in the fires of everlasting hell.*"

She had heard those words before. They'd been uttered with Julie's dying breath moments before the fire brigade arrived.

Nadine raised her head and howled her shame for the second time.

This time, no fireman wrapped her in a blanket and led her away. This time, no neighbors gathered, shocked and stunned at what was happening. This time—

Another shift, another change.

The air was thick and stiflingly hot. She couldn't see through the tears in her eyes. Couldn't breathe through the choking fumes. Pain seared her legs. She smelled burning flesh. She screamed and cried out, writhing as the flames and the stench of her own burning flesh overtook her.

She reached out her hand to the distant, shadowy figure who stood in the doorway, laughing. Laughing through the roar and crackle of the blaze that consumed her. The fire was deafening, ferocious but couldn't drown out that laughter, or the words that followed.

"This is what you left me to, Nadine. You shall feel the pain I felt and know there is nothing you can do to save yourself."

"Julie, help me!"

Again that awful laugh. *"I'll not spare you any more than you spared me. What did it feel like? Deserting your lifelong friend because you might spoil your perfect looks? You killed me, Nadine. Now it's your turn."*

She saw her hand blister, the flesh melt away from bony claws, fierce shards of pain ripping through her soul. This was how Julie had died, tormented.

Nadine was screaming constantly, her terror fueling the demonic laughter. More flames edged toward her, hungry, licking at her seared flesh, causing fresh waves of agony until she was praying for death to release her. *God help me. Help me!*

Her hair was ablaze, its beauty destroyed, and her eyes were beginning to boil in their sockets.

And that was all.

Gary

Shivering, Gary looked around. He was wearing the same clothes as at Erin's party. A light summer suit and open-necked shirt were all well and good for a sultry summer evening but hardly fit attire for a freezing night of sleet and snow.

What the hell was he doing here anyway? He recognized this place as the same street where he'd hit the boy. The houses were still boarded up, and the area seemed exactly the same as it had that night.

The icy sleet slashed down from a dark, wintry sky, and he hugged himself, trying to retain what little body heat he had left. His mind raced. Who had brought him here? Where had Erin's dinner party gone? What was going on? When was this nightmare going to end? And, above all, why was this happening?

Who? Where? What? When? Why?

The streetlamp illuminated the quiet street, and the sleet glittered in its glow. A car's motor hummed, coming closer. After another moment, its headlights made a feeble attempt to pierce the swirling sleet. The car wasn't speeding, so he had plenty of time to get off the street and onto the sidewalk.

At least he would have, if only his feet would work. He wriggled, but found he was rooted to the spot. Breaking out in a horrified sweat, he looked down at his shoes, which seemed frozen to the surface below. The more he tried to shift them, the more they became stuck, as if nailed to the asphalt.

The car was inching closer. A big car. Like his Volvo. A lot like his Volvo.

He bent, determined to get his feet out of those damned shoes and free himself. If he could, he'd be able to run to the safety of the sidewalk before that car mowed him down.

"I wouldn't bother if I were you. It won't make a scrap of difference."

He saw a pair of women's boots in front of him, flat-heeled and practical.

He looked up from his crouched position. "Who are you? What do you want? Why am I here?"

The woman looked familiar but it wasn't until she spoke again that he remembered. "So many questions, Mr. Duncan. Or perhaps I should call you Mr. Westwood? Did you give my son a chance to ask any questions? If you'd phoned for an ambulance as soon as you hit him, the doctors said he might have survived. But, no, you were too concerned about your stupid career, you drunk bastard!"

A groan escaped Gary. He dragged his body upright, aware the car had stopped maybe a hundred yards away. "I didn't know. I swear I didn't know. I tried to find a pulse. I thought he was already dead."

"He had a fractured skull and he was more dead than alive but they might have saved him. You gave him no chance. No chance at all. He was my *life*. He was all I had left of his father."

Tears mingled with sleet poured down Gary's face. He was freezing but ignored it; it was nothing compared to his shame and guilt.

That night was happening all over again but, this time, he was not alone.

"What happened to your son's father?"

"Killed in Iraq. He was in the army. When he died, all I had was Patrick and *you* killed him. You took away my only reason to live."

Gary reached out to her but she backed away. "Don't come near me, you murdering bastard. You didn't know you had my blood on your hands as well, did you?"

He dropped his hands. "What?"

"When they told me Patrick was dead, I couldn't bear it any longer. I wanted to be with my son and my husband, so that same night, I took an overdose of the sleeping pills the doctor had given me."

"Oh my God, no!" Somewhere, on the edge of his consciousness, he heard the car engine start again.

"As I felt myself slipping away, I cursed you, Gary Duncan. Cursed you with my dying breath and now I'm here to watch you die. Alone. And finally I will have my revenge for that young life you so casually snatched away."

"No, please, not casually. I never meant for it to happen. It was an accident. If I could go back again, I swear I'd do the right thing. I'd call an ambulance. Turn myself into the police. Anything, so he wouldn't be dead. You have to believe me."

"You'd been drinking. You were using your phone. What kind of *accident* is that?"

Before he could answer, she was gone, and the car was building up speed. He still couldn't move his feet. He tore at his frozen shoelaces with stiff fingers, but the car was almost on him. His Volvo. The driver was that woman, Patrick's mother.

Then he saw her passenger.

Himself.

Maggie

"*Maggie, my little Maggie May. Home at last.*"

If she opened her eyes, she'd see something other than Erin Dartford's dining room. She knew where she'd be. That voice told her everything. She had lost her mind completely and was reliving a time in her life more than ten years before. Liam's gentle Irish brogue was distinctive, and he was the only one who had ever called her "Maggie May."

She breathed deeply and raised her eyelids.

She was in their bedroom, and Liam was propped up in bed. He looked deathly ill, his head skull-like. Skeletal hands played with the sheet. It had irritated her, that gesture of his. He only started doing it in the last few months of his life, and she had often wanted to scream at him to stop. He was smiling at her, a rictus grin.

She ran her tongue over her lips but her mouth was arid. "I know this isn't happening. Not really."

"Oh, but it is, Maggie May. To be sure, it is all too real."

"Don't call me Maggie May. Only Liam calls me that and he's dead."

"But I am Liam, me darlin', as you well know."

She grabbed a book that was lying on the bed and flung it against the wall. It banged a dent into the plaster. "*No*, you are *not* Liam. You can't be. Liam's *dead!*"

The figure in the bed gave a deep sigh and, with difficulty, pulled the sheets aside. "Why don't you stop all those tantrums and come into bed with me." He patted the space next to him. His pajamas hung off him, and he smelled as if he had wet himself.

She backed away. "No, I won't. You're not Liam. My mind is playing tricks on me. I must be ill. I need to see a doctor. I—"

"Oh, my poor little Maggie May—"

"I told you not to call me that!"

The sick man threw back his head with astonishing vigor and started to laugh. It was raucous and intensified in volume so much that she had to clap her hands over her ears, which threatened to burst with the sound. As she watched, his face began to fill out. Color washed back into his cheeks, and his whole body seemed to be regenerating. The sparse hair became more luxuriant, and the gray faded to be replaced by the ash blond she remembered.

But she was growing weaker. She could feel the energy draining out of her body. Her joints ached. Her spine was bending and twisting, her knees buckling under her weight. *What is happening to me?*

Liam cast aside the remaining covers and sprang out of bed. She stood mesmerized as he came toward her, pity in his soft brown eyes.

"Poor little Maggie, whatever has happened to you?" She let him take her hand and lead her to the dressing table, but found she could only walk with great and painful difficulty. Surely she used to come up to his shoulder. Now she was a good three inches shorter, her body bent and twisted. A wave of excruciating pain struck her, and she cried out with the agony of it.

"Poor little Maggie May," Liam whispered. "Look at yourself."

She stared at the reflection in the mirror of a hunched old woman with a face covered in cancerous growths. She was almost completely bald, and what little hair that remained was gray and lifeless.

She opened her mouth to protest.

The reflection aped her, but the woman she was looking at had no front teeth.

Maggie moved her tongue.

The reflection copied her.

She was looking at herself, at what she had become. She tried to scream but could only manage a pitiful mewling. Her rheumy eyes pleaded at Liam's reflection.

He wore a triumphant smile. "We had better get you into bed, hadn't we? Don't want you dying on the floor, do we?"

"Why?" she croaked, her body screaming in pain.

Liam lifted her into the bed and tucked the stained sheets around her. "Why? Well now, that is a good question, isn't it? I shall tell you why. Revenge, Maggie. I've waited a long time for this. You left me when I needed you most. You knew how ill I was and that I was going to die in a few days. The doctors had said as much. I begged you to let me die at home. I always had a horror of hospitals and nursing homes. And you knew that. God knows I'd had enough of them anyway. It was such a small request, but you wouldn't even do that for me."

"But I had to go to Hollywood … If I hadn't gone then, I might have lost the deal." Her voice was barely a whisper, coming in gasps.

His eyes flashed. "Oh no, Maggie, you may have salved your conscience with that all these years but that isn't how it was, and you know it. You couldn't wait to get rid of me because you wanted me out of the way to be with your lover. He didn't last long though, did he?"

"You knew about Marty?" She was shocked that he knew that secret.

Liam nodded, his expression hard and angry. "Oh yes, I knew all about Marty and you. I knew about the lies you told him. You let him believe I had encouraged you to be with him and that I had insisted you go to Hollywood with him to sign that deal. The truth was that I hated you going and I begged you to stay with me those last few precious days. But you knew that if you didn't go, you might not get a chance to see your lover for weeks because he was going to be working in Australia. That was the only time *he* could go with you. You lusted after that man so much you couldn't even wait a few more weeks, could you?"

Daggers of pain were stabbing through her body. Her throat was closing, and talking was next to impossible. "How … did … you … know?"

"Not important. You're dying now and you haven't got long to go. Soon you'll be lying in your coffin, all alone in the dark."

She shivered.

Liam laughed. "Oh yes, you're scared of enclosed spaces, aren't you? We always had to leave the landing light on and you would never go into the cellar for fear the bulb might shatter and you would be left alone in the dark."

Through the searing pain, panic rose as a memory shrouded her. When she'd been six years old, she'd crawled into a cupboard under the stairs at her grandparents' home. The door had stuck closed behind her, leaving her trapped inside. She'd screamed for help, but her parents and grandparents, thinking she'd gone to bed, were playing whist in the living room.

With the door shut, they couldn't hear her shrieks and crying until a couple of hours had passed, and her mother had left the game to go to the bathroom. When they'd dragged her out, she was hysterical and had wet herself.

Ever afterward, she was claustrophobic and even the thought of being trapped in a small, dark place could make her sweat and lift the hairs on the back of her neck.

Her body was beginning to shut down. Pain was twisting her into a fetal position. Liam's voice seemed to be coming to her through a mist. What little reason she still possessed tried to tell her that this was a horrible illusion and that, at any minute, she would be back at the dinner table enjoying her beef carpaccio.

"No, you can't go yet, Maggie. I haven't finished with you." Liam bent over her and she could smell his hot, fresh breath, in stark contrast with the rancid stench rising from her body.

"You didn't even hang around long enough to see them take me to the nursing home. You didn't even say good-bye. Three days was all I lasted, and when my poor wasted body finally gave up the struggle, I cursed you with my dying breath. All alone in that ugly little room, I swore I would have my revenge on you. It was worth waiting all these years. You will suffer the fate you dread most. Good-bye, Maggie. *Now* I'm finished with you."

She closed her eyes, expecting this horror to end, one way or the other. Either death would claim her as a merciful release or she would be back at that dinner table. She waited. The pain intensified but ...

... She couldn't move or even cry out. What was happening?

She felt herself being jostled about, lifted, and was aware of the murmur of conversation but couldn't really hear it. She tried to blink, but her eyes were sealed shut.

Everything seemed to slow down. Became quiet. Still. Cold.

Again she tried to open her eyes and, this time, found she could, but was trapped in complete darkness. She struggled and gasped, trying to move. Her limbs banged against tight walls.

Panic overtook her twisted, maimed body. She tried to scream, but couldn't. No sound emerged from her crippled throat. She could barely breathe. She tried to kick, to act, to escape, but her body was almost totally paralyzed.

It took her an hour to die.

Sixty minutes was a long time, alone in the darkness of her coffin.

Nick

Nick was sitting on the floor. The threadbare carpet was filthy, covered in crumbs and other detritus, the origins of which he didn't wish to contemplate. The room smelled fusty, along with another rank odor that he realized with horror was himself.

He was wearing dirty, torn jeans and a grimy T-shirt, spotted with food and dribble stains. He tried to stand on achy legs, and his foot kicked a bottle. It rolled away, showing a vodka label. He steadied himself on the arm of a chair that looked as if it might give way under the pressure. His head throbbed with nausea. His stomach heaved and he tasted bile. He had a raging hangover but didn't remember getting drunk at Erin Dartford's party.

He staggered to the grimy window and peered out, the weak sun stabbing his eyes. Shielding them, he squinted at his surroundings. He was in a tiny apartment in a rundown part of town. All around him were gray, unloved buildings, identical, with the unmistakable look of council flats.

Gypsy Farm. *What the hell am I doing here?*

He gripped the window frame, then realized that the familiar weight of his watch was gone from his left wrist. Where was his Rolex Oyster? Not only was his wrist bare, but the pale pink band marking its place, where the sun from those many Mediterranean holidays never managed to penetrate, was gone and his skin was uniformly pale and pasty.

Worse, his wedding ring was gone. *I've been mugged. Someone has mugged me, stolen all my money, and left me here.*

But when had all this happened? Quitting the disgusting living room, Nick entered the equally nauseating kitchen. Dirty plates were piled high in the sink, and the cooker was rank. Out of the corner of his eye he saw something scuttle for cover under the rusting fridge. A cockroach. He shuddered.

He had to clean himself up and get out of here. Find his car. Drive home. Find out what in God's name had happened to him. Had he been kidnapped and held for ransom? It was possible. He was certainly worth a bit. And what if someone had hit him from behind? Maybe he was suffering from amnesia. That would explain why he couldn't remember getting here. He gingerly felt around his head, examining himself for bumps or bruises. Nothing.

Raps on the front door froze him in place. Who could that be and what did they want? Reason told him that if he was being held captive, they would surely have had a key. Maybe his visitor could tell him what was going on. Or, better still, get him out.

He shuffled to the door, on weak, disobedient legs, his head throbbing mercilessly, and opened it.

There stood Deanna, looking horrified at the sight of him. Behind her was a man Nick didn't recognize.

"My God, Nick, look at you. Have you no pride left?"

He tried to throw his arms around her but she jerked away. Of course. He stank. Why would she want to get close to him? He stood back to let them in, wondering who her companion was. Protective, he was watching Nick very warily and kept a cautious hand on Deanna's arm at all times.

"I don't know what's happening, Deanna. What am I doing here? We were at Erin Dartford's table, eating dinner, and the next moment I was here in this god-awful state. What happened?"

"Two bottles of cheap vodka a day, losing the agency. Does that give you any clue?"

Nick stared at her. "What are you talking about? I haven't lost the agency. We're in the top twenty."

Deanna laughed. "Not anymore you're not, and haven't been for the past three years. Nestfield, Harvey, Morton hasn't even existed for the past eighteen months. After what you did, the remaining partners had to sell out to WPP. Don't you remember any of this?"

He slowly shook his head. His addled brain struggled to make sense of it and failed miserably. "Who are you?" he asked the stranger, whose face reflected both pity and contempt.

"You know perfectly well Roger's my husband."

"Your *what*? He can't be. You're married to *me!*"

Deanna's laugh turned even more unpleasant. "That booze really has screwed up your mind, hasn't it? We were divorced over a year ago. I couldn't take any more of the late-night calls from the police. Fishing you out of some gutter or other. I threw you out a long time ago, Nick, and it was the best day's work I ever did."

"Come on, Deanna," Roger said. "There's no point in wasting any more time here. He's beyond hope."

Nick's confused brain couldn't take anymore. He lunged at Roger who stepped back. Nick overbalanced and fell on the floor, his head an inch from the brick hearth. "You bastard! I'll kill you. Stealing my wife!" He tried but failed to get up. Neither Deanna nor Roger made any effort to help him.

Roger reached into his pocket and withdrew a wallet stuffed with notes. He counted out a handful of twenties and threw them down. "Use this to clean yourself up. And if you can find any remaining morsel of self-control, try not to drink it all. That's the last you're getting, though. Don't come begging for any more."

Deanna cast him one last contemptuous glance before turning to leave, a last waft of her signature Armani Code perfume lingering in his nostrils, momentarily masking the stench of his apartment.

Nick struggled to a sitting position, put his head in his hands and wept.

The days and nights blended into one long nightmare. He lost track of time as his body cramped and shivered with withdrawal symptoms. Frightening hallucinations seemed so real they left him sobbing and pleading for mercy. Giant insects crawled up the walls, across the bed, over his arms and legs, leaving him sweating and heaving in a stinking mess. He didn't remember the trigger that had started him on this rapid downward spiral, but it was clear to him, in his more lucid moments, that he had consumed vast quantities of alcohol over a considerable period. His joints ached and his mind begged for vodka, beer, anything.

But he resisted. He still had all of Roger's money but he was determined. *I'm going to fight this.* The only food in the house had been a tin of Spam, an unopened packet of crackers, and a jar of cheap strawberry jam, but he was rarely hungry enough to eat even a few of the crackers. His body craved only alcohol, and his stomach heaved up bile even after a glass of water.

Maybe a few days or even a week went by when, one gray morning, he woke up and realized his head wasn't aching, but his stomach was growling. He was starving.

Stiff and sore, he clambered out of the reeking old bed. But his mind seemed clearer, and he was able to walk rather than stagger. He switched on the kettle and poured a mug of hot water, which he sipped slowly, nibbling on half the tin of Spam. He would have eaten it all but knew that his stomach had been deprived of food for so long, it would probably reject the lot if he gave it too much in one go. No, he would save the rest of that tin for later.

With food inside him, he was already feeling stronger. A new resolve enveloped him. Today was the day he would start the long climb back. Today was the day when he would start to take his life back. Today was the day he'd start to find the answers.

He started by trying to clean the place up but found the boiler didn't work; the dirt and grease simply wouldn't shift with cold water, so he set to boiling kettle after kettle until the sink was empty and all the pots were washed and left to drain. He found an ancient vacuum cleaner that got the worst of the grunge off the carpet until the money ran out in the electricity meter. So he'd have to go out and find a local shop where he could use some of Roger's money to buy more meter cards. And food.

Rummaging around, Nick pulled out some relatively clean jeans and a shirt and, after braving a freezing shower under a nozzle that barely dribbled, he tied his now clean but still unkempt hair back.

He studied his haggard face in the mirror. *I look sixty.* His beard trailed down to his chest. It was gray, but try as he might, he hadn't been able to find scissors or a razor. He gathered up the few meager clothes he could find, along with dirty bed linen and blankets and shoved them in a black rubbish bag that was in the kitchen cupboard. He planned to search for a Laundromat.

He located his keys on the mantelpiece and a relatively clean, if thin, overcoat in the tiny hall. After putting it on and picking up the black bag, he took a deep breath, opened the door, and peered out at the shabby street.

Coils of barbed wire decked the tops of high walls, the sparse grass was covered with dog feces, and the streets were a swirling mass of litter. Old plastic carrier bags mingled with candy wrappers, fast-food cartons, and discarded cigarette ends.

He knew many days had gone past and, without a TV or radio, he had no idea what the date was. Judging by the absence of leaves on the trees, it was probably late autumn or early winter. It was chilly, too, and the only electric fire in the flat was out of action until the meter was fed.

And apparently he had lost three years of his life. *How can anyone lose three years?*

Turning his collar up against the biting wind, he quickly found a miserable-looking shopping parade where half the shops were boarded up and the other half looked as if they should be. At least the Laundromat was clean and warm, although when Nick asked for change for the machines, the assistant visibly backed away. Burying his shame, he consoled himself. *Soon these stinking clothes will be clean, my hair will be cut, I'll get rid of this disgusting beard, and I'll start my life again. And I'll win Deanna back.*

When he wasn't too far out of it to care, he had thought of little else but his wife, especially since he'd last seen her. Oh, not his wife, his ex-wife, whom he still loved. He'd always loved her. Strange how it had taken all this to make him recognize it. He realized he'd taken her for granted. *Never again, angel. I'll show you the Nick you used to know and love. I'll make it up to you.*

When the old Nick set out to get something, he got it. And the old Nick was returning. He wasn't going to let the small matter of a new husband get in the way. *I'll show you. It's not too late.*

His laundry done, Nick went into the disabled cubicle of the washroom at the Laundromat and washed in the sink, finding fragrant liquid soap and paper hand towels, which he used to pat himself dry. Apart from the coat, which he had also washed, he wrapped the clothes he had been wearing in the black rubbish bag and shoved it in the waste bin, determined not to take anything dirty back to the apartment. His newly washed jeans and T-shirt were a bit creased but at least they were clean, fresh, and dry, as was his coat.

Next he would get his hair cut and beard shaved. He would use some of Roger's precious money for that. Just this once. He would buy a razor and shave every day, like he used to. Like any man with pride and a dislike for facial hair would.

He bought cleaning products and returned home, having successfully avoided the liquor store, and set about scrubbing away the grease and grime his earlier efforts had only managed to skim over. He lit scented candles in the kitchen, bathroom, and living room/bedroom, poured liberal quantities of bleach down the lime-encrusted toilet. Soon, the warming scent of vanilla began to replace the previous stench.

Finally, he stood back and looked around the refreshed apartment and felt satisfied. The place was still a hovel but at least it was clean and smelled good.

After his first good night's sleep in his clean bed, Nick woke with a start and an awful craving. His heart plummeted. Just when he thought he was over the need for booze, it had returned. He'd kill for a shot of vodka. *I must keep busy. Take my mind off it.*

He got up and showered, grateful for the hot water, even if it was only a trickle, before dressing and brewing coffee. Some mail had come through the door, and he bent down to pick it up. Bills. Final demands for rent and rates from the council. He looked at the amount and stared at it incredulously. He owed £750 and realized he hadn't a clue how much he had in his bank account. He used to be worth well over three million but clearly that had gone. Hell, he didn't even know if he *had* a bank account anymore. But, given the state he was in, he was pretty sure there wouldn't be £750 to be found anywhere with his name on it.

In the small bureau in one corner of the living room, a drawer was stuffed with unopened official-looking envelopes. Obviously he had been in denial and had shoved them in there rather than deal with them. *If I can't see them, they don't exist.*

The envelope on the top of the pile had the logo of the bank he had used for twenty years. He ripped it open and stared. He was overdrawn by £250. The notice was a couple of weeks old. Most of the overdraft appeared to be bank charges for direct debits that had been bounced, including the rent and rates he was supposed to be paying monthly. He rummaged further in the drawer until he had located all the bank statements going back nearly three years. The older ones showed a speedy decline but at least he had read those at some stage; the newer ones were still sealed in their envelopes. Sitting at his table, he opened the envelopes and spread the contents out in front of him. Looking at them he could piece together a story, and it was an ugly one.

The first one had his old address, the house he had shared with Deanna. The opening balance was in the thousands, and he could see a regular monthly payment of £7500 going out to his wife. In addition to this, store cards that she used were still being paid by monthly direct debit from his account and, clearly, she hadn't been stinting herself, which hadn't bothered him at the time. So what if she was extravagant? He'd been able to afford it, and he loved her. She looked good. She was worth it. Gradually, as the months went by, the outgoings continued to drain his account because there was nothing, utterly nothing, going into it.

The direct debits started to bounce. The one to Deanna seemed to have stopped a year ago, as had the store cards. They weren't being paid, so probably court action was being contemplated.

The papers swirled in front of his horrified eyes as panic mounted. *I must stay calm and think clearly.* But how was he going to clear his debts? And where was he going to start getting a steady income from?

It appeared he was receiving no State benefits at all and in his financial situation, he should surely have been getting his rent and rates paid by welfare. There was no trace of any of the relevant paperwork in the bureau so Nick assumed he had never applied. He chose that as a priority.

Roger had told him that the handout was the last one, but there had been a fortune in paintings and other works of art in Nick's house. Surely he was entitled to some of that? The burning desire for vodka had been replaced by a burning desire to see Deanna and to start trying to convince her that he had begun the long journey back to recovery. She had loved him once. That couldn't have all evaporated in a couple of years.

Nick folded the statements and replaced them in the drawer. He looked at himself in the mirror. He still looked gaunt. His cheekbones were sunken. His skin was still pasty, but at least he was clean and presentable.

Automatically, he looked at his wrist. *I must get another watch.* He didn't even possess a clock, so spent his life guessing at the time. *Maybe I can liberate a TV and radio. And some decent clothes.*

Perhaps Deanna would still be living in their old house. She'd loved it so much he doubted she would have moved of her own volition. He got off the bus a quarter of a mile away, and the closer he approached, the faster his heart beat.

The church clock chimed eleven, so with any luck Deanna would be on her own, with Roger at work. Nick rounded the corner of the exclusive Mayfair street and saw the familiar tall pillars of the Georgian town house.

After his tap, Deanna opened the door almost immediately, but her face fell when she saw him. "What do you want?"

"Just to talk, to try and understand. Please let me in, Deanna. I've come a long way and I'm still not very strong."

She hesitated, then opened the door wider to let him in, closing it quickly behind him as if she didn't want anyone to see him enter.

Nothing had changed. The house was exactly as it had been except … It had a different air about it, but that was probably Roger's influence.

Deanna led him into the living room, and Nick was delighted to see that all the paintings and sculptures remained. He was happy he'd put the house and so many of his treasures in her name. Throughout his evident decline, at least these had been safe from his creditors. He could sell some of them and make a tidy sum to give him some breathing space while he put his life back together.

"You've cleaned yourself up, I see." Deanna said, an unpleasant edge to her voice, as if she was disappointed. But that was ridiculous, wasn't it? "It won't do you any good," she continued, sitting.

"That's an odd thing to say. What do you mean?"

She shrugged her shoulders.

"Could I have a coffee?" he asked, throat parched.

"I doubt you'll be staying long enough."

This was too much. "Deanna, why do you have to be so unpleasant? I want to understand what happened and try and put it right. I need a bit of help. Please, for the sake of all we meant to each other, won't you help me?"

She stared at him, virtually unblinking, for several seconds before standing. "Roger told you, you're getting no more money from us."

"Oh come on, Deanna. I bought this house and everything in it. I'm entitled to half of it at least."

She glared at him, and Nick recoiled from the sight of her face. It appeared contorted and her eyes seemed to have blackened, but how?

"You'll get nothing from this house." She spoke in a hiss rather than her usual quiet tones. "Nothing at all. Others paid with their lives for what you had. Everything you had was paid for in blood."

"*Blood?* That's crazy. I'm a businessman. An ad man. I'm not the bloody Mafia!"

"You *were* a businessman. You are now a tramp. An addle-brained alkie whose only concern is where his next drink's coming from."

From somewhere, he heard a baby cry. "Maybe that was the case for a while. I don't know because I don't remember anything from the time I was at a dinner party at Erin Dartford's abbey until the time I woke up in that fleapit. But I'm over that. I've cleaned myself up and I'm ready to start building my life again."

The crying was coming closer. The door opened. "I've brought him in to see his mummy," a woman said.

A familiar figure came into Nick's line of vision. "But you're—"

"Yes, that's right, Nick. I'm Erin Dartford. We met three years ago, or a couple of weeks ago, depending on your perception." She gave a chilling laugh and handed the screaming tot to Deanna. She accepted him lovingly, holding him close and kissing the top of his blond head.

Nick stared at Dartford, who stared back. She was dressed exactly as she had been that night, even down to the red nail varnish. And what did she mean by *depending on your perception*? Was it three years or two weeks? It couldn't have been two weeks. Too much had happened. He sank into a nearby chair.

"Oh, Nick, Nick, what a very confused man you are," Erin said, her lip curling around sharp teeth. "I think we had better let him in on our secret, Deanna. And you had better get him a drink. He looks as if he needs one."

"No, I—"

"Don't drink anymore? Oh I rather think you will when you hear what we have to tell you."

The baby had quieted, and Deanna left the room with him.

"Lovely child. Only three months old. And Roger and Deanna are made for each other, don't you think? No, perhaps you don't. But you still think you can get her back, don't you? You still think she was yours in the first place. How absurd! As if someone like Chloe Stone could possibly love someone like you. A murderer in all but name."

"*Chloe Stone?*" This couldn't be right. "But her name's Deanna. She was Deanna Ellis."

"She changed her first name and Ellis came from her first husband. David Ellis was a very nice man but it would never have worked out. They were both far too young, you see. She left him in Australia, right after her sister-in-law died. But you would know all about that, wouldn't you? Laura Stone? The woman who loved you so much she gave up her husband for you. And he loved her so much, he turned to drink and killed himself."

"That wasn't my fault. He could have got over it. Started again."

"Like you did, you mean? When Deanna threw you out?"

"I don't even remember that."

"You don't need to."

Deanna returned with a large tumbler of whiskey in her hand. "I've put Laurence in his crib for his nap," she said to Erin as she handed the glass to Nick. He waved it away. She set it on a small table next to him, and he could smell the fumes, enticing, comforting. Abhorrent.

"How are you getting on?" she asked Erin.

"I think he's beginning to understand."

"She's wrong. I don't understand any of this. Deanna, tell me please. What's going on here?"

"I would have thought that was obvious, Nick. Revenge." Deanna's voice was hoarse with emotion. "I've waited all these years since first poor John and then Laura and Andy died. She loved you so much and felt so guilty at what she had done. You killed them all, as surely as if you had taken a gun and shot them. You could have been honest with Laura and told her it was only a fling. Even when she told John about you, you could have been honest and sent her back to him. He would have taken her back. At any point he would have taken her back."

"I didn't know that. Not for sure. I couldn't turn her out. I felt guilty."

"Guilty? You don't know the meaning of the word. You didn't love her, you used her for sex and you couldn't care less about what you had done to John."

"He was weak. A loser."

"And to the whole world, you are as much of a loser. Look at these articles. I saved them for you." Deanna thrust a scrap album to him and, in mounting horror, he turned the pages. Front page headlines from the last three years, all charting his spectacular downfall. *How Are The Mighty Fallen*, read one, while another led with *Mighty Morton's Multimillion Meltdown*. Page after page, each showing increasingly dissolute photographs.

There he was falling out of a seedy Soho nightclub, another where he was leaving court after losing his company because he'd been sued by none other than Jay van Zandt. His PA was quoted in that one: *"I can't believe he is the same man I worked seven years for."* Sarah, looking sad and dejected, stared out from the newsprint.

Deanna continued, "When Laura died, I vowed to avenge not just her death but John's and Andy's as well. Especially John's and Andy's. They were innocents caught up in your selfish web. I deliberately set out to make you fall in love with me and you did. But I tell you, Nick, every night I had to endure you pawing at me, I was revolted. Only the thought that one day I'd make you pay, kept me going."

"You did a pretty convincing job." He still couldn't believe it.

"Why do you think we never had children?"

"It never happened, I suppose. I know you wanted them."

"Not with you. I would never have wanted a child to have you for a father. To have even one drop of your blood coursing through his veins. Roger's the only man I have ever truly loved. He is the father of my child and the husband I shall adore forever. You, on the other hand … I shall enjoy watching you die, lonely and unloved."

"I'll make it back again, Deanna. I can do it."

"What for? What's the point? You will never have me and you're poison in the City. All the agency doors are shut against you because you disgraced yourself. You swindled Jay van Zandt and he made sure everyone knew about it. You're finished, Nick. Washed up. A has-been of the first order. You're dead to the world and dead to me. Pretty soon you'll be dead to yourself as well and good riddance. I shall be dancing at your funeral. Oh, sorry, I forgot, there won't be one. You can't afford it and I'm not paying for it. They can throw you in the landfill for all I care."

Nick stared at her. He could have wept but he wouldn't let those bitches see him cry. His hand went to the glass of whiskey beside him and he raised it to his lips.

Erin smiled.

When they found him, he had been dead almost a month. The police had to break the door down when the neighbors complained of a horrible smell seeping under their doors.

A young police officer almost fainted when he saw the body. The cockroaches had not been idle.

Erin

At the head of the table, Erin surveyed her guests. A smile twitched the corners of her scarlet lips. They had seen revenge exacted. Deanna had even participated. Each had been patient, waiting for their victims to ascend to the peak of their careers, which made the fall that much more dramatic and their own souls darker, more embittered.

She licked her lips. Soon it would be time. The time she always savored. The time of shock and disbelief for the four remaining guests at her dinner table. They were all gazing at her expectantly.

Waiting for her to make a move and lead them. Much as she enjoyed the power she held over them, she would not keep them waiting any longer. She spread her arms wide. "Come with me, my children."

One by one, they pushed their chairs back from the table and stood. Erin's smile grew broader as a metallic taste filled her mouth, a familiar sensation when she had accomplished a mission. It was a taste of iron. Of blood. Soon Erin Dartford's role would be over, and Sovan the Fallen One would return.

She led them out of the dining room, through the entrance hall, and down the former cloister to the library at the end. Opening the door, she led them in and told them to sit.

She studied their faces. Often, when vengeance was done, she would read triumph, elation, satisfaction, but occasionally she would see remorse. Guilt even. A feeling that the suffering had been too great for the crime. She read all of these emotions today.

First Paul. He looked satisfied. His only sister, Julie, had suffered a terrible death because that selfish bitch Nadine had been worried she might get a little scar. Paul felt justice had indeed been done today.

Her eyes traveled to Deanna—or should that be Chloe? There was elation in her face. Nick Morton never knew until it was too late who she really was. She had dedicated her life to ruining the man who had caused the deaths of her loved ones.

Geoff was settling into one of the winged armchairs. He was clearly triumphant. Ten years he had been plotting revenge for his beloved cousin, Liam's, lonely death. Now it was done.

Finally, Melissa. Patrick Morgan had been her godson and his mother, Stephanie, her best friend. She should have showed satisfaction at least, but instead, she looked troubled. Gary. Of all of them, he was the only one who had shown remorse. If Erin weren't one of the Fallen, she might even have saved him. *Ah well, you can't have everything.*

Erin smiled and her audience blanched. She enjoyed that, enjoyed her power over them. The power to grant their wishes. The power to bring them to her for all time.

"My children, it is time for you to speak. For each one of you to tell me what is in your heart. Paul, you shall begin. Tell us all why you summoned Sovan the Fallen One, and why you sought vengeance."

Paul Kelly stood and inhaled deeply. "Nadine Cornwall was a selfish, egotistical cow who deserved to die. She left my sister to burn to death and I have hated that woman for five years. My sister cursed her with her dying breath and she came to me in a dream the night after she died. She told me she would not rest in peace until I had avenged her death. But she told me she was patient and that she was prepared to wait so that true retribution could be made. She told me that I must summon Sovan the Fallen One and do her bidding. I did so and I did as you instructed. I made contact with the bitch, took over her financial affairs, flattered her, made her feel loved." He paused, and his expression changed to a grimace of disgust. "I detested every miserable minute of her company. But it was worth it. Worth every second to see her suffer."

He bowed to Erin, who stretched out the hand with the magnificent ruby ring. He bent to kiss it before resuming his seat.

"You waited five years for your revenge, Paul. I know at times you wanted it over with so much more quickly. I told you revenge is always sweeter when it is left to grow, to mature. When served up in a heated rush, it is quickly spoiled and unsatisfying. Served cold, it can be savored, tasted, all its many flavors anticipated and then delivered. You saw Nadine's rise to fame, her vanity and her shallowness. You had the pleasure of watching her writhe in agony as that body she cared about so much burned to ashes. Are you avenged?"

"I am avenged. Justice has been done and my sister can rest in peace."

"She is already at peace, Paul." Erin smiled.

Confusion shadowed Paul's face. Had he guessed?

No, they never do.

Melissa looked about to stand but Erin didn't want that. Instead, she motioned to Deanna, who almost leaped out of her chair, a wide smile lighting her face.

"Tell us, Deanna."

"As with Paul, my brother John came to me but it wasn't after he died, it was when Laura and Andy passed over. The very next night, I had a dream and in it John told me that Laura had also cursed Nick with her dying breath. He didn't have to ask me to exact vengeance on their behalf, I was only too willing to do it. I hate men like Nick Morton. They think they can do whatever they want, take whatever they want and never have to pay for it. I was determined I would make Nick suffer in the worst possible way, make him fall hopelessly in love with me, be successful, only to have it all taken away from him.

"John told me to summon Sovan the Fallen One and told me how to do it. I did it that very night. You came to me and told me what I needed to do. I changed my name so there was no chance of him connecting me with Laura. I got the job of PA to his business partner and made sure Nick noticed me. To him, I was sexy and available. He soon took the bait and asked me out. Then I stopped being so available but he saw me every day at work and it drove him mad. He fell deeper and deeper in love until eventually I let him catch me. I played the long game with him but it was worth every minute. And when you bent time tonight, or whatever it was you did, I got what I wanted. Nick died horribly at his own hands. He drank himself to death and good riddance!"

"You think I bent time? How do you know how long you have all been here? Is it two hours? Two weeks? Three years?"

Laughing, Erin watched the guests look from one to another. Melissa shivered. "Oh, my children, time is but an illusion, a transitory thing. We blink and a second is gone. Or maybe a lifetime. Who knows? Was Deanna ever married to Roger? Did she have a child?"

All eyes turned to Deanna. Erin knew that Deanna wouldn't even remember how she'd felt holding her baby. Questions darkened everyone's eyes, but she wasn't about to answer them. Not yet. All in good time.

"Are you avenged, Deanna?"

Deanna nodded. "Yes." She approached Erin, kissed the ring and sat.

"Geoff."

He stood and came toward her, three pairs of eyes following him. "Maggie got what she deserved. Liam and I grew up together in Ireland when my parents died. He was more like a brother than a cousin. I left to come to London and a year later he followed me. A few years after that, he met Maggie and fell in love. I never met her because, by that time, my work had taken me to New York. I always meant to come over and visit but never got around to it. It's something I shall always regret.

"Then he called me to say he had been diagnosed with an inoperable brain tumor. He only had a matter of weeks to live. He sobbed on the phone, saying it would be the last time he ever spoke to me. That Maggie was putting him in a home. I was outraged and demanded to speak to her but he wouldn't let me. He told me her mind was made up and that she was going to Hollywood that very day. She could have put it off but she wanted to be with her lover. I rang the airline and booked myself on a flight two days later but as I was leaving for the airport, another cousin called me and told me he was dead.

"That night Liam came to me in a dream and begged me to exact vengeance. I was all for punishing her then and there but I did as he wished. He told me to summon Sovan the Fallen One. I did so and learned to be patient, to bide my time. Her affair fizzled out very quickly once her lover was thousands of miles away in Australia. But a new and attentive man arrived, notebook and pen in hand and apparently desperate to please her. I can't believe how easy she was to deceive. All it took was a few magazine articles praising her novels and she fell into my arms. And you used your influence to ensure they were published."

Erin held up her hand. "You did that yourself, Geoff. I merely showed you the way."

"Like Paul, I hated every lousy second I spent with her. I nearly blew it all wide-open tonight. I couldn't wait for it to be over. To see her suffer and die. I'm glad she's dead and I'm glad she found out how Liam must have felt, all alone and forgotten."

"Are you avenged, Geoff?"

"Yes, I am avenged." He kissed the ring and returned to his chair.

All eyes were on Melissa. Erin noticed she seemed to have shrunk back in her chair, trying to make herself as small as possible. *Now it's time.*

"Melissa. Come to me."

She reluctantly let go her rigid grasp of the armchair and half stumbled to her feet.

"You seem troubled, my child."

"I am. I … I think that, in the end, Gary showed guilt and remorse for what he did. I don't think he deserved to die like that. There, I've said it." She turned to face her fellow guests. "I'm sorry, everyone. I can see why you're happy with what has been done here tonight but I really don't think Steph wanted it to end this way. Not when he was so genuinely sorry. I think she wanted him to pay for his crime by owning up to it and taking the punishment, not by dying like poor Patrick did.

"I could have turned Gary in to the police when he brought his car to our garage. I wish I had, instead of telling all those lies and living a sham life all these years, letting him think I loved him. It was cruel, heartless, and I'm ashamed of myself." No one said anything, and she turned to face Erin.

Frustrated, Erin asked, "Did you have a vision of Stephanie the night she took her own life?"

Melissa nodded.

"And did she beg you to summon Sovan and exact revenge for her death and the death of her son?"

She lowered her gaze. "Yes."

"Did you not think you had a duty to perform? Did you not in fact pursue that duty right up until the end?"

Melissa met Erin's eyes again. "Yes, but I have hated living this lie all these years. Gary's not a bad man. Not really. He made a terrible mistake. Now *this* has happened; it doesn't seem right."

Erin stared at her. She was losing Melissa, an unfamiliar result that didn't please her. "You know that he was in the car, next to Stephanie, when it happened?"

"And he was also on the road. I don't understand that. How could he be in both places at once?"

"He wasn't." Erin wasn't about to explain. "Are you avenged, Melissa?"

"I—"

"Are you avenged?"

"Yes, I suppose so. But I don't take any pleasure in it."

"You are alone in that." Time to cut her losses. Erin did not offer her ring to kiss.

Melissa retreated to her chair.

"My children, all but one of you is satisfied. My work is almost done here and it is time for Erin Dartford to leave us forever. To the rest of the world, it will be as if she never existed. All memory of her will be erased."

The walls, even the foundation of the abbey began to shake.

Deanna screamed. "My God, it's an earthquake!"

Pictures shook and fell from the walls. Cracks appeared in the plaster, which began to flake and crumble, exposing brick. Books fell off shelves, and the very shelves themselves buckled and tumbled.

From the hall, the noise of glass chandeliers crashing to the floor penetrated down the passage and through the door.

The guests were shouting and hysterical, tugging at the door handle but it wouldn't shift.

"It's locked!" Geoff cried. "For God's sake, let us out of here. We're all going to die!"

Erin began to laugh at the irony. "For *God's* sake? No, Geoff, God does not enter into this. I am Sovan the Fallen One. I do the bidding of Lilith, the First Woman. In *her* name, and hers alone, do I work."

Erin saw Melissa and Deanna, whimpering and clinging to each other. Geoff and Paul were white-faced and clearly terrified.

Flames shot from Erin's eyes, blinding, white-hot daggers of light. Her body was enveloped in a bright aura that shimmered and rippled as she writhed and moaned in the ecstasy of it. This was the time she loved most. When her real form took hold once more and she could cease pretending.

All efforts to escape were abandoned as they witnessed her demonic transformation. As the flames of light licked at her lovingly, she watched the humans cower together as her skin transformed into fluorescent scales of green and blue before a golden skin grew over them, coating her. She became taller, her black hair longer, flowing behind her as if blown by a sharp wind.

Gradually, the flames of light subsided, and the tremors slowed to a murmur. Her eyes returned their normal, piercing blue, and she was dressed in a shimmering gold gown with golden amulets on each arm and a serpentine necklace adorning her neck.

Still the four guests huddled together, too terrified to move. Erin Dartford was gone. Sovan the Fallen One, Handmaiden to Lilith the First Woman, stood before them. She was beautiful, but cold and merciless, with no trace of humanity.

Still, the sounds of the abbey falling into ruin echoed all around them as if some clock was running backward, to a time before Erin's restoration work, when it had lain derelict for years.

She spoke and her voice was deeper, more resonant than before. "My children. It is time. The price must be paid. Once, millennia ago, I was the handmaiden of the Goddess of Retribution, Nemesis. I was at her right hand when she exacted justice for heinous crimes, but I wanted more and fell out of favor with her. She tossed me into the great abyss and I became known as the Fallen One. I roamed the underworld for centuries until Lilith found me. She it was who took me as her Handmaiden and since that time I have done her work. I exact vengeance, but my favors do not come for free. I do not act out of righteous anger but out of revenge. Hard, cold revenge. No one ever asks the price of that revenge. None of *you* ever asked me. But now you shall find out."

She saw them cling to each other even tighter and lifted her eyes upward. She opened her arms wide and felt herself grow, expand, transform anew, treating her terrified audience to images forming on her body.

Three of them would see their loved ones in fields of sheer beauty, laughing, happy, finally at peace. They'd feel compelled to walk toward them. Despite what she'd said, none of these three felt frightened anymore, judging by their expressions and actions. Their loved ones were beckoning to them, and they wanted to be with them. Deanna half ran to be with John, Laura, and Andy. Geoff's face lit up at the sight of Liam, fit and well, waving at him. Paul was laughing at Julie who was holding a glass of wine out to him.

Only Melissa held back.

Melissa

Melissa could see all their images, but there wasn't one for her. She watched as Sovan's arms enfolded them into her and stared in horror at another transformation.

The idyllic scene had changed. Geoff, Paul, and Deanna were writhing in a dark pit, filled with hideous creatures that reminded Melissa of a Hieronymus Bosch vision of hell. Some were half-formed imps with twisted faces, some half skeletons, others with bleeding eyes, some with beetle-like carapaces and pincer-like claws. They scurried around the screaming trio, spitting, jabbing at them with long, thin spikes, drawing blood. Deanna was hysterical. Geoff and Paul were trying to claw their way out. But it was too late. Sovan's arms closed around them and they were gone.

Melissa continued to watch Sovan who stood still, arms at her sides, gazing into the distance. She seemed to be waiting, still bathed in a greenish glow which illuminated the shattered room.

A low rumbling started beneath Melissa's feet. Trancelike, she tore her gaze away from the statuesque figure and looked down. The polished parquet floor was breaking up from the force of the tremors. Any second now that floor was going to erupt. She could feel the tremors growing stronger, her fear growing greater.

Something's coming. But what?

She had to get away. To safety. Everywhere she looked, the room was wrecked. The lights were long gone. If it weren't for the green glow, Melissa would be in total darkness.

Two figures glided closer to Sovan. The two waiters were dressed very differently from the livery they had been wearing at dinner. They wore tunics of bronze and carried staffs of ebony, topped with precious jewels. Rubies danced in Sovan's glow. They took up a position either side of her.

A fresh wave of terror sent Melissa dashing for cover behind a threadbare winged chair in the darkest corner of the room. The tremors grew fiercer, and every bone in her body was vibrating.

Something—or someone—was going to arrive at any moment.

Thankfully, none of the three seemed even vaguely aware of her presence. Maybe she was not important to them. Melissa certainly hoped so. Hiding behind her chair, she hoped and prayed they would forget she even existed.

Another low rumbling began, gradually building to a roar as the floor exploded on the far side of the room. Lightning bolts shot upward. She cowered still further behind the chair, terrified of what would happen next. Her heart thumped in her ears and the tiny hairs on the back of her neck and on her arms stood on end. Yet, scared as she was, she could not tear her gaze away from the unfolding scene.

A figure was forming, the figure of a woman. And, as it grew in substance, the ghastly trio bowed their heads.

The tremors died away and the noise ceased. "Hail Lilith. Hail Queen of Darkness." The voice was Sovan's and was echoed by the two men.

The figure had fully formed and Melissa stared, transfixed. Like Sovan, she was tall and beautiful. But her beauty was more frightening than Sovan's. Even from across the room, Melissa could see her eyes glittering red in the demonic green light in the room.

Those eyes found her. Melissa held her breath. She felt them bore into her and, inexplicably, leave her.

"You have brought fresh souls to me, Sovan. You have served me well."

"One remains."

"I have seen into her soul. She is not mine. You shall return with me."

Sovan and the men bowed again and approached Lilith. The green light surrounded them, covering them in a pulsing blanket that throbbed faster and faster. A pounding emanated from it. Lightning shot upward once more. Then, total darkness.

She was alone.

After minutes of silence, she eventually dared to stand up and felt her way round the chair. A cold breeze blew through the broken windows and chilled her. How much time had passed? Maybe not very long. But, given Sovan's earlier trickery, Melissa didn't know whether this was even the same night. It was still pitch-dark outside, without moonlight to illuminate the room.

Without any light at all, she doubted she could find her way to the door. She couldn't even trust herself to get to a window to clamber out. Even though she was on the ground floor, she would need to climb up on something to reach one, and she doubted anything in the trashed abbey was fit to take her weight, assuming she didn't sever an artery on the broken glass that littered the floor and the sills.

Leaning against the chair, which groaned under the pressure, Melissa tried to calm herself and decide what to do. Sovan had said that all memory of Erin Dartford would be erased so that explained why the abbey had reverted back to its former ruined state. *But if all memory of her is erased, how is it that I can still remember her? And what do I do now? Where shall I go?* With a rush of panic, she realized that her old life was gone forever. She didn't love Gary, had never loved him, but they had lived together for a long time.

Everything was over. She had no home and no job. Struck by a wave of hopelessness, she sank to the floor and wept.

Through her tears, Melissa saw the room start to brighten. A golden dawn was breaking.

Voices floated to her. The first was sweet and angelic. *"Rest, my little ones. You are home now."*

"It has been so long."

"But it is over at last."

"They paid a terrible price."

"Never ask the price of what you do for love." It was the same angelic voice that had spoken first. Melissa was sure the others were the voices of the dead.

She heard a sound over to her right and turned to see Stephanie smiling at her.

"You did the right thing, Mel. Come with me, we go this way." A door opened. Beyond it was a shining garden, sunlit with the greenest grass and brightest flowers she had ever seen.

She struggled to her feet and ran to Stephanie. "Is it really you?"

"I think you know the answer to that." Stephanie squeezed her hand and the two women embraced.

"Do you know why I was spared?"

"Because you forgave Gary in the end and put a stop to Sovan's plans for him. And he showed true remorse. That is all I ever wanted. The others all had a chance to put things right, one way or another, but they didn't. Nick could have shown regret at what he did to Laura, John, and Andy but he never, even for an instant, felt any conscience for what he had done. Maggie, too, felt nothing but disgust for Liam as he lay there, sick and dying. Nadine didn't try and save her best friend.

"All three did exactly as Sovan hoped, so now they are dead and their souls are hers to serve up to Lilith. Sovan herself feeds on the bitterness, hatred, and vengeance of others. All three of her conspirators reveled in the misery of the horrible deaths of their partners. Their souls were blackened by their lust for vengeance, so Sovan gets to keep them for herself. But she could do nothing with you. Once you showed mercy for Gary, you freed yourself from her control. Lilith saw that and left you alone."

Melissa's mind was in turmoil. So many questions begged to be answered.

"What about Julie, Liam, and the others? Where are they?"

"You saw them. Sovan showed you. That was really them and they are in Summerlands." Stephanie pointed through the doorway.

Melissa marveled at the beauty she saw. Rolling grassland and bright sunshine. Crystal waterfalls flowed, and butterflies in many vivid hues fluttered and darted from flower to flower.

"They are free now," Stephanie said. "In their case, they were truly wronged and justice needed to be done. Nemesis fought for them, and for me, and won."

"Surely they must feel desperately sad. After all, their loved ones were only doing their bidding, as I was doing yours."

Stephanie stroked her arm. "You heard the angel, Mel. You never ask the price of what you do for love. In the beginning, all of you had doubts. Most of you wanted to avenge your loved one's death quickly but Sovan persuaded each of you to wait. We had died horribly and tragically, uttering curses with our dying breaths. The price of those curses was to be denied everlasting peace. Our curses pawned our souls to Lilith and her Handmaiden Sovan, until a terrible price was exacted. Maggie, Nadine, and Nick paid that price today. Geoff, Paul, and Deanna put them there. At any time, they could have stopped it. They could have exercised their free will as you did. But they were all too far gone."

"But their partners showed no remorse. Gary did. That's why I felt so awful."

"It wasn't just what Gary did. Sovan looked into your soul and saw goodness. She could do nothing with that. When she looked into the souls of the others, she saw only their darkness. They had become truly hers in a way you never did. To Geoff, Deanna, and Paul, it wouldn't have mattered if Maggie, Nick, or Nadine had shown true remorse; they would still have wanted vengeance. It seems harsh I know, but you were never obsessed with the need for revenge in the same way they were. Their hearts were filled with so much hate that there was no hope for them because, somewhere along the way, they lost their humanity. Their loved ones will mourn them, but they will recover in the paradise of Summerlands."

"When you came to me in that dream after you had taken your own life, you begged me to avenge yours and Patrick's deaths and I promised I would. Surely that makes me as bad as they are."

Stephanie shook her head. "No, Mel. Yours was a righteous anger. Theirs was pure hate. The difference is the price of your soul."

Melissa was silent for a moment. She knew what Stephanie said was true. Melissa had been scared witless when Sovan had manifested herself that first night when summoned. She had appeared clothed in gold and bathed in fiery light, and Melissa had been terrified to do anything other than carry out her will.

But her heart had never been in it. Many times over the years, she'd wanted to give up, walk out of Gary's life and start anew somewhere else. But, trapped by her promise to Stephanie, she'd kept going, telling herself that Gary was only getting what he deserved. Tonight, as she had told Sovan and the others that she regretted what she had done, a great weight had been lifted from her. She had felt free for the first time in all these years. Things were going to be very different. Again she wondered what her life would be like from now on. *Life?*

Another realization dawned. "They're all dead and you've come to take me too, haven't you?"

Stephanie nodded slowly. "When the angel came for me, she brought Patrick with her. He had gone to Summerlands the moment he died. He's waiting for us there. Are you ready to cross over?"

Melissa took one last glance backward at the shattered room and nodded. "I'm ready."

Stephanie took Melissa's hand and led her through the door.

Gary

He was back in the car again, in the driver's seat.

One minute he had been on the street, inches away from the bumper, unable to move or avoid the inevitable crash that would maim or kill him and the next he was behind the wheel.

No one was in the passenger seat. No sign of Stephanie Morgan.

The car had stopped.

Maybe it hadn't happened yet.

But the hope crashed and burned as he saw where he'd stopped. If he got out of the car, he would see the lifeless—or, as he now knew, *almost* lifeless—body in the street. Patrick Morgan.

Gary unhooked his seatbelt and opened the car door, putting his cell phone in his pocket. He looked back down the wet street.

The lump lay on the freezing tarmac with sleet raining down on it.

As he locked the door, he saw the street sign. Crimson Street. He remembered that all the streets around here were named after colors, Green, Yellow, Turquoise, Crimson. Some long-ago town planner's idea of a joke, perhaps. They had always been depressing, mean little streets.

He fumbled for his cell phone and took it out. He reached the boy and bent down. He was exactly as before, cold and still. No sign of a pulse, however hard Gary tried to find one. But maybe it was true. Maybe if help got to him sooner, the boy could be saved.

Gary stood and dialed a number. For a second his thoughts drifted back to Melissa, but he could no longer remember what she looked like.

The call was answered on the second ring. He took a deep breath.

"I need an ambulance right away. Crimson Street, Walworth. A little boy's been knocked down and he's not moving." He paused. "And you'd better send the police. They'll want to talk to me ... Who am I?" He sighed. "I'm the driver of the car that hit him."

About the Author

Following a varied career in sales, advertising and career guidance, Catherine Cavendish is now the full-time author of a number of paranormal, ghostly and Gothic horror novels and novellas.

Her novels include: *The Stones of Landane, Those Who Dwell in Mordenhyrst Hall, The After-Death of Caroline Rand, Nemesis of the Gods trilogy: Wrath of the Ancients, Waking the Ancients,* and *Damned by the Ancients, Dark Observation, In Darkness, Shadows Breathe, The Garden of Bewitchment. The Haunting of Henderson Close, The Devil's Serenade, The Pendle Curse* and *Saving Grace Devine.*

The Crow Witch and Other Conjurings is a collection of her previously published and brand new short stories.

Her novellas include: *The Darkest Veil, Linden Manor, Cold Revenge, Miss Abigail's Room, The Demons of Cambian Street, Dark Avenging Angel, The Devil Inside Her,* and *The Second Wife.*

She lives by the sea in Southport, England with her long-suffering husband, and a black cat called Serafina who has never forgotten that her species used to be worshipped in ancient Egypt. She sees no reason why that practice should not continue.

You can connect with Cat here:

Website: catherinecavendish.com/
Facebook: facebook.com/CatherineCavendishWriter
X (formerly Twitter): twitter.com/Cat_Cavendish
Instagram: instagram.com/catcavendish/
Tik Tok: catcavendish
Bluesky @catcavendish.bsky.social

Curious about other Crossroad Press books? Stop by our website:
http://crossroadpress.com
We offer quality writing
in digital, audio, and print formats.

Subscribe to our newsletter on the website homepage and receive a
free eBook.

www.ingramcontent.com/pod-product-compliance
Lightning Source LLC
Chambersburg PA
CBHW022043170626
46808CB00003B/1343